KILLER CHASE

In Suta Springs, Wolf Cotton's simple bank robbery goes wrong. One of his gang shoots the bank manager, Curtis Jordan disappears, but Wolf and Ab Cooper are killed during the getaway. Trigger-happy Drew Hudson gets the loot — yet doesn't make the share out meeting! Curtis vows to find and kill him. Meanwhile, Deputy Danny Ridge wants to discover who gave Wolf Cotton the bank's back door key. The chase is on, but who will get their comeuppance first?

Books by John Davage
in the Linford Western Library:

UNSIGNED AVENGER

JOHN DAVAGE

KILLER CHASE

Complete and Unabridged

LINFORD
Leicester

First published in Great Britain in 2011 by
Robert Hale Limited
London

First Linford Edition
published 2012
by arrangement with
Robert Hale Limited
London

British Library CIP Data

Davage, John.
    Killer chase. - - (Linford western library)
    1. Western stories.
    2. Large type books.
    I. Title II. Series
    823.9'2–dc23

    ISBN 978–1–4448–1310–4

Published by
F. A. Thorpe (Publishing)
Anstey, Leicestershire

Set by Words & Graphics Ltd.
Anstey, Leicestershire
Printed and bound in Great Britain by
T. J. International Ltd., Padstow, Cornwall

This book is printed on acid-free paper

1

Chester Darrow, sheriff of Suta Springs, was roused from his whiskey-induced siesta by the sound of gunshots. Two, to be precise. But that was two more than he would have expected to hear on this steamy, airless, late afternoon when all sensible people should have been taking their nap or attending to their lawful business, not shooting up the damn town!

Chester swore and removed his feet from his desk, knocking a half-empty red-eye bottle to the floor. It smashed, and he cringed as the precious liquid made a dark pool on the stone floor. Fuddled by the effects of the red-eye and slowed down by a double helping of Ma Flint's chicken pie at lunchtime, he heaved himself from his chair and lurched towards his office door. Grabbing his Winchester from the gun rack, he stepped out on to the boardwalk, his head feeling as though it had been kicked by a stampeding buffalo.

The scene that confronted him turned Chester's innards to water. Across the street, three masked men were emerging from the alleyway at the side of the Suta Springs bank, each toting a gun, two of them clasping sacks of money. A fourth masked man sat astride his horse at the mouth of the alleyway, holding the reins of three more mounts.

Chester cursed again and lifted his Winchester. Making a pitiful attempt to aim, he fired as the three men scrambled on to their horses, ready for a quick getaway. Amazingly, considering the sheriff's semi-inebriated state, his bullet took one of the raiders in the chest. A huge thickset man, he was thrown backwards off his horse, dropping the canvas sacks he'd been clutching. One of these burst open and coins and dollar bills spilled out into the dirt. Chester blinked, unable to believe his luck — which, anyway, was about to change.

Another raider, after spurring his

horse into action, turned and fired at the sheriff. Chester felt a searing pain in his shoulder as the slug penetrated. He dropped the Winchester and staggered back, falling through the door of his office.

He was only half-aware of more shots and the thud of hoofs as the remaining three raiders attempted to make their escape. Out of the corner of his rheumy eye he caught a glimpse of his young deputy, Danny Ridge, half-crouched in a firing stance outside the batwings of the saloon, a two-handed hold on his Remington, firing at a moving target. Chester pulled himself upright with difficulty — in time to see a second raider thrown from his horse by the force of one of Danny's bullets.

What Chester observed next turned his blood to ice. A woman, heavy with child, had come out of Doc Palmer's house and had been crossing the street. She was midway across but, terror-stricken by what was happening, stood transfixed in the centre of the road, mouth half-open, eyes wide with fear. Chester was about to shout a warning to her when the woman was hurled to the ground by the forelegs of another raider's horse. Seconds later, another of Danny's bullets took the same horse in the neck. The animal faltered, skewed sideways and crashed to the ground, throwing its rider over its head. The man rolled in the dust, drawing his six-gun in the same movement and firing in the direction of the saloon before scrambling to his feet and disappearing into one of the alleyways off the street.

The fourth raider, riding a black mare with a distinctive white mane, tail and foreleg, and clutching the remaining two money bags, glanced back, then rode away unscathed in a cloud of dust.

*   *   *

People were appearing from buildings, cautiously at first, then with more confidence as they realized that the danger appeared to be over, at least for the moment. Their immediate concern was for the young mother-to-be lying motionless in the street.

A circle of townsfolk quickly gathered round her, faces wreathed with anxiety. A short, stocky man with thinning white hair pushed his way through the throng. Doc Palmer knelt beside the woman for some moments, making his examination, then rose slowly to his feet, shaking his head.

Several of the women in the crowd let out anguished wails and buried their faces in their hands or in the arms of their husbands.

Somehow, Chester got to his feet. His drink-sodden head still throbbing, his hand grasping his shoulder and blood seeping through his fingers, he moved in the direction of the gathering. As he drew nearer, he recognized the young woman lying in the dust. Her neck was at an odd angle and a thin line of blood trickled from her mouth. Her terrified eyes stared unseeing at the sky.

'Julie Chandler,' Chester muttered to himself, a deep feeling of sadness coursing through him.

At that moment a man dropped to his knees beside her and cradled the woman's head in his arm. He was in his early twenties and his eyes were wide with horror.

'Julie, no! No!' he bawled. Then gently, using two fingers, he closed the woman's eyes, sobbing unabashedly as he did so. The man was the woman's brother-in-law, Clayton Chandler.

Another young man, one of the two bank tellers, came down the steps from the bank and walked across to Chester. He was white-faced with shock.

'Th-they shot Mr Hall,' he said, his voice shaking. 'Shot him twice. He's . . . dead.'

Owen Hall was the manager of the bank. *Had been* the manager, Chester corrected himself.

'Bastards!' he said. 'How'd they get in? I thought the bank closed an hour ago. Front doors were shut tight, last time I looked out.'

'They came in through the back door,' the young teller replied. 'Mr Hall must have forgotten to lock it this morning. I guess they planned to tie us up and leave quietly the same way.'

'So why didn't they?'

'One of them got nervous and shot Mr Hall. After that, they just took off — fast.'

Doc Palmer joined them. He addressed Chester, gesturing back at Julie Chandler. 'Looks like a broken neck,' he said simply. 'And a lethal blow to the head.'

'Dear God,' Chester said softly. 'First Boyd loses his son, now he loses his daughter-in-law and his unborn grand-child.'

The doctor nodded. 'And Ada's not long for this world,' Doc said, referring to Boyd Chandler's wife. 'Can't last more than a couple of months. Seems like the whole Chandler family are cursed.'

'Boyd's still got Clayton,' Chester said, looking back at the young man who was cradling Julie Chandler's head.

'Huh!' Doc Palmer gave a sniff of disdain. The two men exchanged meaningful glances but said nothing.

'An' the raiders killed Owen Hall, too, Doc,' Chester said a few moments later.

The doctor's shoulders slumped. 'So somebody needs to tell his wife and young Ellie. Guess I'd better do it.' He glanced at Chester's shoulder. 'Come and see me later and I'll fix that.' Then he turned and walked back towards his house across the street.

Chester looked round to check the whereabouts of his ginger-headed deputy. After a moment he saw Danny examining the body of the first of the two fallen raiders. Chester turned away from the crowd and made his way across.

'Wolf Cotton,' Danny told him, nodding at the body of the thickset raider. He had pulled the man's mask from his face, exposing a heavy black beard. 'Seen his kisser on a law dodger.'

'And the other man?' Chester said.

'The other man's Ab Cooper, one of

Cotton's gang. Seen his face on a dodger, too.'

With an effort, Chester tried to gather his thoughts. 'So one of the other two will be Curtis Jordan,' he said. 'There's never been a picture of him, but he's a known member of the gang.'

'So who was the fourth critter?'

'Don't know,' Chester said. 'Can't be Virgil Cotton, Wolf's kid brother. He was killed a month ago in a barroom shootin' in Tucson.'

'So the fourth man must be Virgil's replacement,' Danny said.

Chester nodded. 'Ain't ever known Wolf Cotton to work with less than three other gunmen in his gang.'

'Well, one of 'em is somewhere in town,' Danny said. He was eighteen years old and had an enthusiasm which contrasted strikingly with his boss's reluctance to get involved in anything hazardous nowadays. 'I got his horse, but he skedaddled. I'd best get a search party organized fast. You get over to Doc Palmer's and get that shoulder fixed, Ches. You've lost a lot of blood, an' it's still leakin'.' He glanced up the street. 'Mrs Chandler?'

Chester shook his head. 'Clayton Chandler's with her. Guess he'll be the one to tell Boyd.'

The two men looked at each other. Neither spoke, but each knew the other's thoughts. Boyd Chandler wouldn't rest until the man who'd mowed down his son's widow was dead and buried.

'Doc Palmer's on his way to see Owen Hall's wife, to break the news that her husband's dead,' Chester said. He looked shrewdly at Danny. 'You want to go with him? Young Ellie . . . '

'Yeah, good idea,' Danny said, moving away quickly.

'I'll see about the search party,' Chester called after him.

2

Twenty miles from Suta Springs in the little town of Red Creek, Herbie Calhoun, owner of the Red Creek mercantile, was watching Kate, his pretty young assistant, closely. He sensed that something was wrong.

Herbie himself was still raw with grief after the death of his wife, just three months earlier. Sixty-eight years old and with no kin to help out, since that day he'd left much of the running of his business to Kate.

The girl was in her early twenties with sky-blue eyes and shiny fair hair. In fact, Kate Hudson had more or less taken over all of the jobs Maud Calhoun had been responsible for, including the accounts. She was quick, reliable and completely trustworthy. That had been Maud's verdict only days after the young woman had started working for them six months ago, and since then Herbie had had no cause to disagree.

Kate's other talent was drawing. Maud had discovered this when she'd spotted a sketch Kate had done of Herbie.

'Why that's *exactly* the way he looks when he's thinking,' Maud had said, laughing. 'You've caught him perfectly, Kate.'

Herbie smiled to himself remembering. Afterwards, Maud had insisted on having the sketch framed, and it still hung on the parlour wall in Herbie's house.

But today he knew that Kate was having difficulty focusing on the columns of figures in the accounts book. And he knew why. She was worried about that kid brother of hers. Whereas Kate was clearly as decent and virtuous a young woman as you could wish for, Drew Hudson was as devious and slippery as a snake. And, in Herbie's view, just as deadly.

In all the time Kate and her brother had been in Red Creek, Herbie had never known Drew to do an honest day's work. He spent most of the time holed up in the Green Garter saloon, playing poker and losing most of the money Kate earned.

★　★　★

Herbie was right about Kate. She *was* worried. Drew had been gone a week now, and there'd been no word. Not that this was particularly unusual. Her brother had a habit of disappearing for several days at a time, gambling, whoring, or chasing some money-making scheme or other.

It always ended in trouble. Six months ago it had been a woman — the wife of a prominent town councillor. The councillor had discovered that Drew had been sleeping with his wife and he'd threatened to kill Drew if he and his sister didn't get out of town fast. They had.

Add to that the brawls in various saloons, the near shoot-outs, the hanging-out with nefarious characters who lived on the wrong side of the law — Kate had lost count of the number of times they'd had to make a hasty exodus to avoid the consequences of Drew's misdeeds.

But this time she had an especially bad feeling. Not least because of those three men Herbie had seen him talking with over at the Green Garter.

'Nasty lookin' bunch,' Herbie had told Kate. 'Especially the one with the bushy black beard. Mean-lookin' critter, but seemin' to like what Drew was tellin' him. Coulda been because Drew was plyin' him with red-eye. And the other *hombre* and his buddy looked no better. Just stared silently at Drew the whole time I was watchin' 'em.'

Kate had asked Drew about it later that evening, but he'd immediately become defensive.

'Just three fellas,' he'd said. 'We had a few drinks, kinda friendly-like, an' we talked. Herbie should keep his bald head out of my business!'

Kate hadn't been satisfied, but the more she'd questioned him, the angrier he'd become, finally shouting at her to 'shut the hell up!' before storming out of the room.

That had been three weeks ago. But in the period between that day and a week ago, Drew had been edgy and keyed up. She had said nothing, hoping that whatever it was he was planning would become evident without her asking about it.

But it hadn't. And then he'd told her he was going away for a few days, and that when he returned they'd have more money than they'd ever dreamed of. And, no, he couldn't tell her about it just yet, but she had to trust him. Which had only served to make Kate even more worried.

Now, staring at the columns of figures in the Red Creek mercantile accounts book but not seeing them, she just knew something bad had happened.

'You OK, Kate?' Herbie asked her suddenly.

She jumped. 'What? Oh, sure, Mr Calhoun.'

'Nothin' wrong? Only you're lookin' a little pale.' He put a hand on her shoulder.

'I'm fine,' she said.

'You know you can talk to me if you've got a problem.'

Kate forced a smile. 'Sure, I know. Thanks, Mr Calhoun. I'll have these figures ready for you in half an hour.'

'There's no hurry,' he assured her. 'Ain't seen Drew for a few days.'

'He's — he's away,' Kate said.

'Anywhere special?' Herbie probed.

'He's looking for work at one of the ranches down south,' Kate replied.

It was a lie. And she felt sure that Herbie knew this. Even so, he just nodded.

'Let's hope he finds something,' he said. 'You heard from your aunt lately? The one in Latimer?'

'Yes,' Kate said, brightening. 'I had a

letter a couple of weeks ago.'

'She still want you to go and stay with her?'

Kate nodded. 'She'd like that, but it's seventy miles away and — well — I'm happy here.'

Herbie smiled. 'That's good to hear, Kate.'

She didn't tell him that Aunt Bella's invitation hadn't included Drew, and that was the reason she wouldn't be going.

Where are you, Drew?

3

Curtis Jordan was long-legged, skinny and fast on his feet. After dodging the bullet from that young deputy, he had bolted through the backstreets of Suta Springs and was now holed up in a rat-infested barn on the outskirts of town. Near the derelict building were the remains of a burnt-out homestead, long since abandoned.

He decided to wait until after dark before venturing back into town to steal himself a horse and make his final escape.

What a fiasco the bank raid had turned into! Curtis remembered Wolf's last words before they had entered the bank.

'This one should be easy. We're in an' out of the back door, quiet as mice. But if anythin' goes wrong an' we have to separate, we meet back at the cabin,

OK?' He'd looked directly at Drew Hudson. 'You reckon you can find it again, kid?'

'Sure,' the kid had said.

Well things sure as hell *had* gone wrong. Starting with the shooting of the bank manager. The idiot had gone for the shotgun he'd kept under the counter. Wolf had been about to club him with his pistol when that damn fool kid had got trigger-happy and shot the banker — *twice*!

'What'n hell you tryin' to do?' Curtis had snarled at him. 'Rouse the whole damn town?'

'I-I thought — ' the kid had begun.

'Let's get out of here!' Wolf had barked, snatching up two of the money bags they'd filled. The kid had grabbed the other two. Wolf looked at him. 'I'll deal with you later.'

Except that there hadn't been a 'later' for Wolf. He'd been shot dead, as had Ab. And he, Curtis, had only got away by the skin of his teeth. But who had got clear? That damned kid! And with two bags of the loot!

Curtis had never liked him. The kid had spun a yarn, had been a fast talker, and Wolf — still vulnerable after the death of Virgil — had been fooled. Both Curtis and Ab had tried to warn him about the kid's lack of experience, but you could never shift Wolf once he'd made up his mind. Besides, something about the kid had reminded Wolf of Virgil, and that had been enough. That plus the fact that Wolf always liked to work with three others. Reckoned four was his lucky number.

Some luck!

Suddenly, Curtis heard movements and soft voices outside the barn. He glanced quickly around, then made a dive for a heap of straw and buried himself in it.

Moments later, the two men came to the barn door and pushed it half-open. Curtis couldn't see them, but he could hear them talking.

'Careful, Joe,' one of them said.

'Don't worry,' the other replied. 'I

ain't aimin' to get myself killed.'

'Gonna search it?'

'No, I ain't. The critter could be pointin' his firearm at us right this minute.'

'But Chester said — '

'Listen, Harry, I know what Chester said,' Joe replied. 'But I got a wife an' kids, an' I aim to go home to 'em tonight. To hell with Sheriff Chester Darrow and his 'we can smoke him out, boys' speech.'

'Ain't a bad idea, though.'

'What?' Joe said. 'What you talking' about, Harry?'

'Smoke him out. In other words, set fire to the barn. Then we just wait until he comes runnin' out.'

'Are you crazy?' Joe said. 'Sure, he'll come runnin' out — if'n he's in there — with two guns blazin'. And we'll be crow meat! Come on, let's get back to the horses.'

Curtis heard them walking away and smiled to himself. Maybe he wouldn't have to wait until dark and creep back

21

into town after all.

Moving swiftly, he pushed the straw heap aside and made for the half-open door, pulling his six-shooters free as he ran. The two men hadn't reached their horses and had their backs to the barn. They heard Curtis crash his way out of the building but were much too late to draw their own weapons before the gunslinger ploughed two bullets into each of them.

Curtis grinned. 'Now I've got myself a horse. Ain't that nice?'

* * *

'Dead? Both of 'em?' Chester stared at his deputy.

Danny Ridge nodded. 'Outside the barn at Kelton's old homestead. Sid Pitman found them half an hour ago. He got worried when neither of them met him in the saloon like they'd arranged, and he went lookin'.'

'Kelton's barn,' Chester repeated.

'Yeah,' Danny said. 'Reckon that's

where the raider was holed up. He took Harry's horse and skedaddled. We'd best get a posse together, Ches.'

'Too damn late now,' Chester said. 'Be dark in half an hour, an' there's no moon tonight. Too much cloud. We'd never get the fella's trail, if'n he doesn't cover it anyways.'

'In the mornin' then,' Danny said. His tone became impatient. 'We've gotta do *somethin*', Ches. Can't just sit on our hands.'

Chester moved papers around on his desk and avoided the eighteen-year-old's eye. His shoulder hurt like hell, even though the doc had patched it up, and he was gasping for a shot of red-eye. Didn't want to take it in front of Danny, though. 'Sure, sure,' he said. 'In the mornin'. You sent Howard out there?' He was referring to the town's undertaker.

Danny nodded. He perched on the edge of Chester's desk and the sheriff groaned inwardly. The youngster had something on his mind and seemed bent on voicing it regardless.

'What is it, Danny?' Chester said. 'What's eatin' you?'

'I talked to Ellie earlier.'

'How was she? And her ma?'

'Mrs Hall's under sedation. Doc Palmer gave her somethin' after he broke the news about Owen.'

'And Ellie?'

'Ellie's kinda numb with shock. Even so, I asked her about her pa, an' she's positive Owen wouldn't have forgotten to lock the back door of the bank. She reckons the raiders had a key. Either that, or somebody let 'em in. An' I agree with her.'

Chester felt sick. His mouth was dry and he seemed to have no spittle to moisten it. This whole damn business was turning into a nightmare. But townsfolk, and especially Boyd Chandler, would be expecting him to sort it out, and the last thing he needed was *complications*.

'Now, hold on,' he said. 'Are you sayin' somebody local helped the

Cotton gang rob our bank? 'Cause if'n you are, I don't believe it. Wolf Cotton don't need no help robbin' banks, him an' his gang have been doin' it for a long time now.'

'Would have been nice an' easy, though, if one of the gang hadn't got trigger happy,' Danny said.

'How d'you mean?'

'They could've been in an' out of the back door with no interruptions. Could've tied up Owen and young Fisher and Jones, the tellers. It would've been hours before anybody might have thought to go lookin' for 'em. Wolf an' his gang would have been long gone.'

Chester succumbed, his thirst getting the better of him. He took a bottle of red-eye and a glass from a drawer and set them on the desk top. His hand shaking, he poured a shot of the life-saving liquid into the glass, downed it in one, then poured another. Danny watched him with disdain.

'So who'd you reckon did it then?' Chester scoffed. 'The mayor? One of the town councillors? Listen, Danny. Tomorrow we see if'n we can pick up that raider's trail, although I reckon we'll end up chasin' our tails, 'cause Wolf Cotton's men have never been known to leave a trail before. Even so, we'll go lookin'. What we *don't* do is go stirrin' up a hornet's nest by goin' round town accusin' folk. Now go home an' get some sleep.'

Danny sighed and slid off the desk. 'OK, Ches. I'll be back first thing.'

Chester watched him go, shaking his head slowly. The kid was too keen by half. Too eager to look for *complications*. Life was tough enough without *making* problems.

He downed his drink and poured himself another.

★ ★ ★

Danny left the sheriff's office and walked towards his room at the back of the feed store. Lucas Smedley let him have it for a dollar a week, having taken a liking to the young man.

Both Danny's parents were dead. His pa had been killed in the war and his ma had died eight years later, worn out from trying to scrape a living on the homestead she and her husband had set up after their marriage. Danny had been twelve years old then. A skinny, not to say malnourished, kid with a complexion the colour of cold porridge. He hadn't stayed but had lit out to seek his fortune — at least, that's what he'd told himself. After working as a barroom swamper, a cowhand, and riding shotgun on stagecoaches, he'd finally ended up in Suta Springs — now a sun-bronzed whiphard figure of a young man, older than his years in outlook but not yet cynical about life's unpredictability.

What had kept him here? Two things. A job as deputy sheriff, which nobody else seemed to want. Probably because they didn't fancy working for a drunk. And a girl — a Miss Ellie Hall.

Danny had been smitten the very first moment he had laid eyes on her coming out of the bank with her pa. Pretty as a picture in her straw hat and lacy pink dress. That had been six months ago. But before he'd screwed up enough courage to make some sort of approach, Clayton Chandler, brother-in-law of the woman killed by the raider's horse, had moved in on her. Now Chandler and Ellie were courting, Ellie having been swept off her feet by the slick-talking Mr Chandler. At least, that's how Danny read the situation.

Earlier, when he'd gone to the Halls' house with Doc Palmer to break the bad news, Ellie's heart-shaped face and chestnut curls had quickened his pulses yet again. The pain of missed opportunity stabbed at his innards for the umpteenth time.

But after the doc had gone, having given Mrs Hall a sedative, Danny had lingered. Stumbling over his words at first, he had somehow managed to ask Ellie whether it was like her pa to forget to lock the back door of the bank. And she had been unshakeable in her opinion.

'Pa took his job seriously,' she said. 'He would never have been so neglectful as to leave the back door of the bank unlocked.'

'So they had a key,' he said.

'They must have,' she said.

'But how did they get hold of one?'

'I don't know.' Her eyes misted with tears. 'He was a good man, Danny. He didn't deserve to die like that.'

At that moment, Danny had wanted to take her into his arms and comfort her, but he couldn't bring himself to do it.

'I'm so sorry, Ellie,' he said. 'We'll do everythin' we can to get the critter who — who did it.'

There was a dubious look in her eyes as she replied. 'You and that drunk, Sheriff Darrow? I don't think so, Danny,' she said bitterly.

'*I'll* try, Ellie,' Danny said. 'You have my word on it.' She was silent for a moment, then she put a hand on his arm. 'Thank you,' she said simply.

He had left her then, his heart aching

with love for her — a love he cursed himself for being unable to express. But he was also filled with a determination to carry out his promise to Ellie. Somehow, he would track down her father's killer. According to the description given by the young bank teller, Owen Hall's murderer had not been Wolf Cotton or Ab Cooper, but one of the two raiders who had got away.

And in spite of Chester Darrow's dismissal of the possibility, Danny was convinced Wolf Cotton had had a helper, and that the helper had been somebody local.

He knew who he *wanted* it to be. The man who had stolen his girl. Clayton Chandler. And it could easily be him. After all, he could have somehow got hold of Owen Hall's keys whilst paying a call on Ellie. Taken them, made a duplicate of the key to the bank's rear door, then returned them before they were missed. It would have to have been done over a weekend, when the bank was shut, but that wouldn't have been impossible.

Question was, why would Clayton Chandler help Wolf Cotton rob the Suta Springs bank? For a cut of the money? It didn't make sense. The Double C was a successful ranch, wasn't it? Boyd Chandler was a rich man and, after Scott Chandler's death, Clayton was Boyd's only heir.

Danny climbed the steps to his room at the back of the feed store. OK, so it wasn't going to be easy, but he was determined to find out the truth of the matter. For Ellie.

4

At 6 a.m. the following day, Kate Hudson was awakened by the sound of drawers opening and slamming shut. In the half-light of early morning, she could just see the stooped figure of her brother cramming things into two sacks.

'Drew?' She rubbed sleep from her eyes. 'Where have you . . . what are you *doing*?'

'Gettin' out of here,' he said. 'We both are. Get dressed.' His face was streaked with prairie dust, his blond hair stood on end and there was a hunted look in his baby-blue eyes.

The room Kate and her brother were occupying, rent-free, was at the back of the store and was one of two rooms used for storage. Herbie Calhoun had cleared it so that they would have somewhere to sleep and put their things until they could get a place of their

32

own. It was sparsely furnished, and washing facilities was a pump in the yard behind the shop. Herbie himself still lived in the neat little house he had shared with his wife, two streets from the store.

'Oh, Drew,' Kate said, sighing. 'What have you done now?'

'Got us a heap of money, that's what,' he replied. 'Only we can't stay in Red Creek it's too . . . too near.'

'Too near to what?'

'Suta Springs.'

Her eyes narrowed. 'What's in Suta Springs?'

He laughed. 'The bank I robbed yesterday,' he said, matter-of-factly.

She stared at him. 'You robbed a *bank?*'

'Me and those three guys Calhoun saw me with in the Green Garter.' Drew grinned. 'They were the Cotton gang.'

Kate suddenly felt sick. 'Where — where are they now, these three men?'

'Dead,' Drew said, after a moment. 'Don't worry, I spent most of the night coverin' my tracks.' He threw an empty carpetbag towards her. 'Get packin'. I'll tell you the rest when we're on our way.'

She frowned. 'I don't have a horse. Remember? We sold mine when we arrived here.'

'Me neither. I just sold mine to Walt Hatch at the livery.' He chuckled, 'Dragged him from his bed to do the deal. He weren't too happy about it until he figured he was gettin' a good deal.'

'Why did you sell it?'

'The horse kinda stood out in a crowd, with all those white markin's,' Drew told her. 'Somebody might remember it.'

'So how are we travelling?'

'We're borrowin' Herbie Calhoun's buckboard.'

'Stealing it, you mean.' Kate put her head in her hands. 'Oh, Drew, things were going so well here for us.'

'For you, maybe,' he said. 'There's

nothin' here for me. We can make a fresh start somewhere, now that I've got money.' He grinned again. 'Eleven thousand dollars and some small change! I counted it earlier. Now, hurry. Get dressed and be ready to go in ten minutes. I'm going to get Calhoun's buckboard.'

'But where are we going?' Kate wanted to know.

'Latimer,' he said. He looked at her. 'Aunt Bella's always askin' you to visit, ain't she?' He grinned crookedly. 'I read those letters she sends you when you ain't around.'

She stared at him. 'How do you know she'll have us?'

'She doesn't have to have us, we've got enough money now to get a place of our own,' he said. 'Now get movin'. I want to be out of here pronto, before anybody comes lookin'.'

Kate watched him leave, then started to dress herself. 'Another day, another town,' she muttered to herself. 'Will it ever stop?'

* ★ ★

Curtis sat in the empty cabin and built himself a smoke. Somehow he hadn't been surprised to find it empty when he'd arrived. He'd had a feeling that the kid would have done a runner with the money. Still, he'd had to check.

The cabin was a low-roofed run-down shack near some old mine workings at the foot of a rocky drift of hills. Wolf had found it some months ago, occupied by some old-timer. The place was a perfect hideout but, naturally, the old-timer had been reluctant to quit his isolated but comfortable home, so Wolf had been forced to kill him. Now, the early-morning sunlight made a pale rectangle on the floor in front of the open door. Outside, the horse Curtis had acquired was feeding on the sparse patches of grass surrounding the cabin.

It had been a long night's ride, and Curtis reckoned he could risk a short sleep before moving on. He'd taken the extra time to carefully cover his tracks, but now he was bone tired. He needed to give his horse a rest, too.

He knew exactly where he was going. To Red Creek, where they had first met up with Drew Hudson. Curtis seemed to remember the kid saying something about a sister who was working in the mercantile there. Likely, then, that Drew would return there, or at least send word to his sister to let her know where he was.

One thing Curtis was sure about. Wherever Drew Hudson was hiding, Curtis would find him and take his share of the bank raid.

And then he would kill the kid.

5

Late afternoon in Suta Springs and Danny Ridge sat in the sheriff's office staring at a law dodger with Wolf Cotton's face staring out of it. In the cell out back, Chester Darrow was sleeping off the effects of eight hours' hard riding. Fruitless riding, as it had turned out. A heavy storm had wiped out any tracks either of the raiders might have left — and Wolf Cotton's men were famous for covering their tracks anyway — and the posse had returned, dejected, an hour ago. It was pure speculation where the raiders might be now.

So the best bet of making any progress on finding them depended on finding the identity of the person who had helped the gang, Danny reckoned. The person who had supplied the key to the back door of the bank.

He chewed his bottom lip, trying to make a connection between the bearded outlaw in the picture and Clayton Chandler. But there was no obvious tie-in between the two men.

Even if Danny had wanted to discuss his ideas with the sheriff and maybe formulate a plan of action, it would have been impossible. Right now Chester's snores were building to a crescendo and the likelihood of him waking in the next hour or two was remote.

Which was why Danny decided to take matters into his own hands. He pushed the law dodger back into the desk drawer and stood up. He would go and talk to Clayton Chandler. He'd seen the other man earlier, smartly suited, ready for Owen Hall's funeral. But that wasn't for another hour, and the likelihood was that he was in the saloon taking a drink.

Which proved to be the case.

Chandler was sitting at a table by the window, a bottle of red-eye and a shot glass in front of him. He was staring out into the street, a faraway look in his eyes.

A guilt-ridden look?

Danny got a beer from the barkeep and walked over to the table. He pulled out a chair and sat down.

'Howdy,' he said.

Clayton Chandler looked up without speaking. He appeared less than pleased to see the young deputy.

'How's your pa?' Danny asked.

The other man's face took on an even bleaker expression than before. 'He's real tore up, like you'd expect.' He stared out of the saloon window, then muttered, 'It should never have happened that way.'

Danny immediately picked up on the odd choice of words. 'How d'you mean? 'That way'.'

'What? Oh, I mean . . . me havin' to watch Julie die.'

It still seemed a strange thing to say, but Danny let it go. 'How come you were in town? Business?'

Clayton glanced at Danny, then looked away. 'Yeah, I needed some things from the store. Never got around to pickin' them up in the end,' he added quickly.

The two men concentrated on their drinks for the next few minutes, then Danny said, 'Strange how the raiders were able to get in through the back door of the bank, don't you reckon?'

Clayton shrugged. 'Guess Owen forgot to lock it for once. Happens when you're gettin' on a bit, an' he was no spring chicken.'

'So Wolf Cotton an' his boys just got lucky, that what you're sayin'?'

'Guess so. Prob'ly would've just shot the lock off the door had it been locked.'

Danny shook his head. 'Unlikely. That would have roused half the town before they'd even got started. No, I reckon they had somebody to let them in.' He looked directly at the rancher. 'Or they had a key.'

Clayton poured himself another shot and gulped it down. 'Yeah, well, I gotta be goin'. It's Owen's funeral soon an' I aim to be there to support Ellie.' He gave a crooked smile. 'Reckon you missed out there, Ridge. Ain't no secret you'd taken a shine to Ellie Hall. Didn't make your move fast enough. Still, the best man won, ain't that right?'

Danny felt a stab of jealousy at the mention of Ellie's name. 'Don't know about 'best man',' he said. 'Seems to me she drew the short straw. 'Sides, she agrees with me about the bank raid. Reckons her pa wouldn't have forgotten to lock the back door of the bank. Reckons the raiders had a little local help.'

Clayton Chandler's face took on an ugly look. 'Listen Ridge, just stay away from Ellie or it'll be the worse for you. You hear?'

'Reckon not,' Danny said. 'In fact, maybe it ain't all over between me an' her. Maybe I'll still have a chance when I track down her pa's killer *an' get the name of the critter who helped the gang.* Reckon she'll look more favourably on me then, don't you?'

Clayton Chandler stood up, knocking his chair backwards. 'I told you to stay away from her!' he yelled.

He launched himself forward, grabbed a fistful of Danny's shirt with his left hand and backhanded the young deputy across the mouth with his right. The blow split Danny's lip. A second blow caught the side of his head before he could respond.

Danny staggered back under the impact but managed to stay on his feet as Chandler came towards him. This time, when a punch came, Danny stepped inside of it and grabbed Chandler with both arms, tripping him with a backward heel. The two young men fell to the ground and rolled over.

Danny was first up, and he hit Chandler before the other man could get his hands up to shield his face. Blood spurted from Chandler's nose but he continued to move forward in a rush, throwing punches. Danny dodged them easily, sinking a wicked punch to Chandler's stomach and following it up with a crashing blow to the other man's head.

Chandler staggered backwards, blood from his cut eye and smashed nose pouring down his face and on to his white funeral shirt. He blinked several times, took in Danny's threatening pose and the avid gleam in the young deputy's eye — and decided he'd take matters no further.

He pulled a handkerchief from his jacket pocket and mopped the blood from his face. 'I gotta get to Owen Hall's funeral, but this ain't finished, Ridge,' he said.

'Any time you like,' Danny told him.

He watched as Clayton Chandler slunk out of the saloon.

'Any time at all,' he said to himself.

6

On a morning two days after the bank raid, Boyd Chandler walked away from the Suta Springs graveyard. It stood atop a hill on the north side of the town. Behind him, a flower-covered mound and a simple cross marked the burial place of his young daughter-in-law and unborn grandchild. Next to it, another wooden cross marked the grave of his dead son. Two more appropriate and substantial gravestones would replace the crosses later.

Ahead of him, a small group of townsfolk wound their way down the hill, followed by Clayton Chandler and by Monte Doyle, foreman of the Double C ranch. Ellie Hall hung on to one of Clayton's arms, as if in danger of collapsing before they reached town. Only the evening before, she had attended her father's funeral with her mother, the mayor and most of the town's businessmen. Boyd, who had also been there saying a last goodbye to his old friend, had noticed the giveaway facial marks of his son's fight with Deputy Danny Ridge. Boyd had guessed the fight had had something to do with Ellie Hall. It was no secret that the young deputy had had designs on the banker's daughter before Clayton moved in.

Boyd, although only too aware of his son's shortcomings, had been pleased at the possibility of having Ellie, the daughter of his best friend, become part of his own family.

Clutching Clayton's other arm was Boyd's wife, Ada Chandler. Ada had always loved Julie, right from the time she and Scott had been childhood sweethearts. And after Julie's parents had died of the fever, when Julie was just fifteen, Ada had taken her in and treated her like a daughter. Now Ada herself was a sick woman, reduced to almost a shadow, and Boyd had the feeling that Julie's death, so soon after that of Scott's, would be the finish of her. Scott had died in a riding accident, six months ago, just days after learning that he was to become a father.

Boyd was tall, lean and muscular, with high cheekbones and a deep forehead. He wore a black suit and a black sugar-loaf Stetson. Under the hat, his face was etched with a mixture of grief and anger, and his grey eyes were filmed with tears.

The townsfolk continued their melancholy procession down the hill. But one person had separated himself from the small crowd and had hung back to wait for Boyd to catch up. Boyd saw that it was Chester Darrow. The sheriff was running the brim of his hat through his fingers and staring worriedly at Boyd.

'It's a sad day, Mr Chandler,' he said, as Boyd reached him.

Boyd gave a curt nod and eyed Chester with a look of contempt. It was barely ten o'clock in the morning, yet he could smell whiskey on the sheriff's breath.

'Listen,' Chester said. 'I know you think I should've done more to find those two remainin' varmints but, like I told you, the trail petered out after that storm. 'Sides, they'd taken care to cover what tracks there would have been.'

'So you said,' Boyd answered.

He had no confidence in Chester Darrow. The man just wanted a quiet life and a full bottle of red-eye. His deputy, young Danny Ridge, was more diligent, but Chester kept him on a tight rein, not wanting to be shown up by the young man's enthusiasm.

After a moment, Chester shrugged and walked on. Boyd watched him, a sour feeling in the pit of his stomach.

Clayton waited for his father, leaving Ellie and Monte Doyle to walk on with Ada Chandler. He was a good four inches shorter than his older brother had been. His black suit seemed to hang loosely on his frame and there was a bleakness in the grey-green eyes that peered out from under the grey Stetson. He seemed to have had little sleep since the bank raid, Boyd observed. Then he remembered that Clayton had been almost the first person on the scene after Julie had been mown down. Had watched her die, in fact. Boyd guessed it was the kind of shock that haunted your dreams for a long time.

'How's Ellie?' Boyd asked.

'Like you'd expect after buryin' her pa yesterday,' Clayton replied. 'Her ma couldn't face comin' here again today. She sends her apologies.'

Boyd grimaced. 'Owen was a good man and my oldest friend. Didn't deserve to die that way.'

'Why'd they have to kill him, for Chrissakes?' Clayton said abruptly. 'Wasn't it enough just to take the money?'

'Accordin' to that drunk Darrow, one of 'em panicked when Owen went for the shotgun he kept under the counter,' Boyd said. 'One of the two that got away. An' Darrow's given up the chase.'

Clayton sighed. 'Guess that's it, then.'

'Like hell it is!' Boyd snapped. 'Somebody's got to find those two critters an' either kill 'em or bring 'em back here to hang!' He stared at his son. 'An' it can't be me, with the way your ma is now.'

The two of them looked at each other, saying nothing but reading each other's thoughts. Ada Chandler wasn't long for this world.

'Wh-what you sayin', Pa?' Clayton said.

'I'm sayin' for once *you're* gonna act like the man I've tried to bring you up to be,' his father told him. '*You're* gonna go after those two critters an' avenge your sister-in-law's death, and the murder of my best friend.'

⋆   ⋆   ⋆

Before catching up with Ellie, Clayton stared after his father as the latter strode off in the direction of the town.

His eyes narrowed.

It was no bad thing that his father had suggested he go after Curtis and Drew. He had planned to do that anyway, suspecting that Danny Ridge intended to go on a single-handed manhunt. Clayton wasn't interested in catching Curtis Jordan or Drew Hudson, but he was keen to stop Danny Ridge catching them and extracting from them the information that he, Clayton Chandler, had helped them rob the Suta Springs bank.

But then again, if he came back from a manhunt without either of the raiders, his father wouldn't be satisfied. As soon as Clayton's mother had passed on, Boyd would set off on his own manhunt. And if he ever caught Curtis or Drew alive and they talked . . .

The thought chilled Clayton to the bone.

He came alongside Ellie and she grasped his arm. Her tear-stained face looked up at him from under the veil of her hat. Stray wisps of chestnut-coloured hair escaped from under it.

'Monte's taking your mother back to the ranch, Clayton. I . . . I need to get home.'

He nodded. 'Sure, I'll walk you there.'

They were silent for some minutes as they made their way in the direction of Ellie's home.

'I don't understand it,' Ellie said after a while, voicing a train of thought that had been going on inside her head. 'Pa was always so meticulous about things like that.'

'Things like what?' Clayton asked.

'Locking doors.' She shook her head. 'It wasn't like him to be careless.'

Clayton felt his heartbeat quicken. 'What d'you mean?'

'The back door of the bank,' Ellie said. 'It was how the raiders got in. I've been asking questions and it seems the bank had been shut for best part of an hour, the front doors locked tight. They went in through the back door, and that's made of steel, like the front doors. They didn't break in, Clayton. Young Fisher, the teller, says they just opened it and walked in. So it was unlocked.' She looked up at Clayton again. 'I don't understand it,' she repeated.

Clayton avoided her eye. 'Ain't no good frettin' about it now, Ellie. What's done is done. Guess your pa got forgetful for once in his life.'

'And the raiders just got lucky?' Ellie shook her head firmly. 'I don't believe it. They knew they were going to be able to get in that way.'

'How?' Clayton asked, after a moment. He could feel a cold sweat breaking out on his brow.

'They had a key. Or somebody unlocked it for them,' she said. 'Danny Ridge thinks so, too. But I doubt if he'll be able to persuade Chester Darrow to investigate further.'

Ridge, Clayton thought. Damn him! The bastard was still trying to set Ellie against him and move in on her.

'What're you sayin'?' Clayton asked, his mouth suddenly dry. 'That somebody in Suta Springs helped the raiders? Who? And how would they get a key?'

'I don't know,' Ellie answered. 'If Danny ever catches up with that Curtis Jordan, maybe we'll find out. Danny wants to know the truth.'

And that mustn't happen, Clayton thought.

7

Forty miles away, in Red Creek, Curtis Jordan was entering Herbie Calhoun's mercantile. An elderly woman who was just leaving the store glanced in his direction, saw the wintry look on his face, and hurried out into the street.

There was a pungent smell of tobacco and herbs as Curtis pushed his way through farming equipment and racks of working clothes to get to the counter.

He stood for a moment, lighting a thin, black cheroot and staring at Herbie, who was looking back at him across the counter. Something in Curtis's eyes sent a chill down Herbie's spine.

He had recognized him the moment Curtis had come into the store. He was one of the three men Drew Hudson had been talking with in the Green Garter some weeks ago.

Drew Hudson.

There was a bitter taste in Herbie's mouth as he thought of Drew and Kate Hudson. The way they had upped and left without a word, stealing his buckboard into the bargain — why, it wasn't Christian! Hadn't he and Maud taken them in and given them a place to stay, and Kate a means of earning a living? And the two youngsters had treated him like that! He got a sharp pain in his gut every time he thought about it.

'What can I do for you, mister?' Herbie said at last. He tried to sound relaxed, but failed.

Curtis blew a curl of smoke from between his lips, then moved forward and leaned on the counter. 'Information,' he said. 'That's what you can do for me.'

Herbie swallowed. 'Well, I'll help if I can.'

Curtis nodded slowly. 'You sure as hell will, mister, otherwise you'll be the late proprietor of the Red Creek mercantile.' He smiled an ugly smile and took another draw on his cheroot. 'OK?'

'OK,' Herbie said quietly. The sudden pain in his gut felt like a knife-thrust and his knees threatened to buckle under him.

'Drew Hudson,' Curtis said. 'Name mean anythin' to you?'

Herbie nodded. 'Sure. I knew him.'

''*Knew him*'. That mean he ain't in town any more?'

'That's right,' Herbie said. 'He left two days ago.'

'Where'd he go?' Curtis asked.

'I-I don't know,' Herbie replied. 'They — he just left town.'

''*They*'. That mean him an' his sister?'

Herbie wanted to kick himself. In spite of the way they had behaved towards him, he didn't want to involve Kate in any trouble Drew might have got himself into. Especially when that trouble seemed to involve a gun-slinger like the man in front of him now.

'I ain't hearin' you, mister.' There

was a warning look in Curtis's eye and he flexed his fingers before putting a hand on his holstered .45.

'Yes,' Herbie said quickly 'His sister.'

'What's her name?'

'Kate.'

'An' you don't know where they've gone.'

'No.'

'That's too bad,' Curtis said.

He reached forward and grabbed Herbie's wrist. Then, taking his time, he stubbed out the lighted end of his cheroot on the back of Herbie's hand.

The store owner cried out at the searing pain and Curtis scowled at him. 'I hope for your sake you're tellin' the truth.'

Herbie whimpered, unable to speak and feeling a sudden dampness at his crotch.

'Yessir, I sure hope that's the truth,' Curtis repeated.

With that, he walked out, leaving Herbie with beads of cold sweat on his forehead and a pain in his gut that seemed about to cut him in half.

He had lied to the gunslinger. He did have an idea where Kate and her brother might have gone. To their aunt, her mother's sister, in Latimer, a town some seventy miles north from Red Creek. She'd said that her Aunt Bella had always wanted her to go and live there. Not Drew, just her. Herbie guessed that the aunt knew what kind of man Drew had become through reading the letters Kate had written to her. Not that Kate would have given her details of Drew's antics, but Herbie guessed that Bella Gower had probably been able to read between the lines and come to her own conclusion about the young no-good.

Had Kate gone to Latimer? Had she taken that no-good brother of hers with her? Or had she gone alone? For her sake, Herbie hoped it was the latter. As long as she continued to try and look out for Drew Hudson, she would be shackled to a life of misery.

And danger.

★   ★   ★

Danny spent most of the rest of that afternoon talking to people in Suta Springs, in the hope that someone would have seen something that would give him a clue to the whereabouts of either of the raiders who had escaped.

He was still hoping for a clue that would make a connection between the robbery and Clayton Chandler, but for the moment he contented himself with trying to learn something about the two escapees.

He was desperate for information. All he knew about them was that they were members of the notorious Cotton gang, and that one of them — probably the one who had holed up in Kelton's barn — was named Curtis Jordan.

But it seemed that most of the townsfolk had either been taking their siestas or minding their own business until the shooting had started. And then only a handful of them had ventured into the street or to their windows to witness what was happening. By early evening Danny was becoming despondent.

'Need a cuppa coffee an' a think,' he muttered to himself, making his way towards Ma Flint's café.

And it was there that he caught up with Ben Whitefield. Ben owned the local barber shop. He was a small man, and bald as a coot. He looked up from the table where he was sitting when Danny came into the café, and he beckoned the young deputy across.

'Evenin', Danny,' the little man said. Lamplight shone on his bald pate as he worked his way through a supper of mutton stew and potatoes. He mopped gravy from his chin with a hunk of bread as he spoke.

Danny sat himself down. 'Howdy, Ben,' he said. 'You wanted me?'

Ben nodded and pushed his plate away. 'Listen, Danny, I don't know if this is gonna be of any help, but I had Leonard Nolan in the chair earlier.'

'From the Diamond Brand ranch?'

Ben nodded again. 'That's him. Well, we got to talkin' about the bank raid and what happened to Julie Chandler.'

'You saw what happened?' Danny said.

'Yeah, I saw it all through my shop window. Scared the hell outa me, I can tell you. I stayed put until the shootin' had stopped.'

At that moment Ma Flint appeared at Danny's elbow.

'Anythin' I can get you, Danny?' she asked.

'Coffee, Ma,' Danny said, without looking up. 'Go on,' he told Ben.

'Well, I was tellin' Leonard all about it, and I got to describin' the horse one of the raiders was ridin'. The one who got clean away. Kinda distinctive, it was. A black mare, with a white tail, white mane and white foreleg.'

'Yeah, I remember the horse,' Danny said.

'Right. Well Leonard reckoned it had been one of his.'

'It had?'

Ben nodded. 'Reckoned he sold it to a horse dealer from Red Creek six months ago.'

'Which one?' Danny asked. 'There are a couple.'

'Man by the name of Hackett,' Ben said.

Ma reappeared with Danny's coffee. She put it on the table and walked away.

Danny hardly noticed. He was staring at Ben.

'Hackett,' he repeated. 'Red Creek.'

'Yeah. Leonard didn't know any more. Got a good price for the horse, so he didn't ask questions.'

Danny sipped thoughtfully at his coffee. 'It's a start. Thanks, Ben. You told Chester about this?'

Ben shook his head. 'Not yet. Reckon I should?'

'No, I'll do it,' Danny said. 'Though I doubt he'll follow it up.'

'But you're goin' to, ain't you?'

'Damn right I am,' Danny said. 'An' maybe I should let Boyd Chandler know I've got a lead that I'm gonna follow up. He's as angry as hell that Chester's given up on the case.'

'Good idea. Boyd deserves any comfort he can get. You know anythin' else about the two jiggers who got away?'

'Only that one of 'em is Curtis Jordan.'

Ben nodded. 'Yeah, I heard that.'

'Don't know for sure which one of 'em killed Julie Chandler, but I'm guessin' it could be him,' Danny said. 'Still, I'm obliged for the lead, Ben.'

'I wish you luck,' Ben said. 'Reckon you're gonna need it. You sure can't expect much help from that boss of yours.'

Danny grinned ruefully, then drained his coffee mug.

8

After leaving the mercantile Curtis Jordan had spent a fruitless time asking questions in Red Creek. Nobody seemed to know anything useful. Sure, plenty of folk remembered Drew Hudson and his sister, but nobody knew where they'd high-tailed it to. Although it was generally agreed that their departure had been sudden.

'Can't say 'xactly why. Guess it was somethin' to do with Drew, an' not Kate,' Polecat, the barkeep at the Green Garter opined. He looked calculatingly at Curtis as he refilled the latter's shot glass with red-eye. 'He always was a tricky customer. But I reckon you might know that.'

Curtis gave him a sharp look. 'What makes you say that?' His voice had a hard edge.

'Didn't I see you an' a coupla other

men talkin' with Drew in here a few weeks back?'

Polecat was a big man, heavily muscled, and not easily intimidated. Even so, he kept a careful eye on Curtis's gun hand. The fact was, he knew exactly who Curtis was, as well as the identities of the other two men Drew had been talking with that day a few weeks ago. Drew, slightly the worse for wear after an afternoon of steady drinking, had told Polecat afterwards. Named each of the three men. Boasted about it, in fact, then swore Polecat to secrecy. They were the Cotton gang — minus young Virgil.

Thus Polecat reckoned he was almost certainly the only person in Red Creek who knew who Curtis was. He had no idea where the other two members of the gang were now, nor did he know the reason why Curtis was so anxious to find Drew Hudson, but he didn't doubt it had something to do with some double-cross Drew had pulled. The kid was stupid enough.

'Yeah,' Curtis replied, after some consideration. 'Yeah, you saw us. What about it?'

'Nothin',' Polecat said easily. 'Just makin' conversation.'

'But you ain't got any idea where Drew and his sister are now?'

'Nope. Why're you so keen to talk to him? He owe you money or somethin'?'

'That's my business,' Curtis told him.

'He was always losin' at cards,' Polecat said. 'Like the other fella who came in occasionally. The one who used to play poker with your buddy with the beard. Reckon that fella could've built up a sizeable marker with the bearded guy.'

Curtis' gazed hardened. 'You notice too much, my friend. Liable to get you into trouble one of these days.'

'Sure, sure,' Polecat said, smiling. 'Like I said, I was just makin' conversation.'

Curtis swallowed his drink. 'Guess I'll stick around for a day or two an' talk to a few other folks.' He glanced up the stairs. 'So I'll be needin' a room.'

'OK,' Polecat said. 'I can fix you up. I — er — didn't catch your name.'

Curtis stared at him for a moment, then said, 'Smith.'

Polecat smiled.

★ ★ ★

It was late that night when a rider — a man who had come through Suta Springs earlier that day — told Polecat about the bank raid in that town.

'Bank manager was shot dead an' a young woman was killed when she was mown down by a raider's horse,' the man told him.

'That right?' Polcat said.

'Yep,' the man said. 'They're sayin' it were the Cotton gang. Two of the critters are dead, but two of 'em got away.'

'Which two?' Polecat asked.

'Curtis Jordan and some unknown guy.'

An' Mr Jordan's sleepin' under my

roof, Polecat thought. An' I reckon the other guy is young Drew Hudson. But he said nothing.

★   ★   ★

Once he'd left Ma Flint's café in Suta Springs, Danny wasted no time before riding out to the Double C ranch to tell Boyd Chandler his plans to follow up the lead Ben Whitfield had provided.

He was ushered into the large ranch house, and into Boyd's study, by the woman who was nursing Ada Chandler. It was a stylishly furnished room with a long leather couch and leather arm-chairs. A longcase clock stood in one corner next to a gun cabinet. Boyd Chandler sat behind a polished walnut desk, a map of the territory spread out before him. The rancher was studying it when Danny walked in.

'What do you want, Danny?' Boyd asked. 'Come to tell me that drunken boss of yours is gonna get off his fat butt an' do somethin' about catchin' my daughter-in-law's killer?'

'Not exactly,' Danny said, nervously. And he proceeded to tell the older man all that he had learned in Ma Flint's café.

'Hackett?' Boyd said, when Danny had finished. 'I've heard of him. Horse dealer, yeah. Reckon he could have been one of the bank raiders?'

Danny shook his head. 'More likely he sold the horse on, and its buyer was the raider,' he said. 'But with any luck, he'll be able to give me the man's name. Then again, Red Creek's only a small place. There could be plenty of folk who'll recognize the description of the black mare and know its owner. I plan on startin' with the livery man.'

'Clayton might've got ahead of you,' Boyd said.

'How's that?' Danny asked, suddenly apprehensive.

'He's gone on the same manhunt as you're plannin',' Boyd told him. 'An' I reckon you could be right about Red Creek. Clayton said he planned to start askin' questions there as he'd heard the Cotton gang often passed through that town an' somebody might know somethin'.'

'Is that right?' Danny said, unable to keep the contempt he felt for Clayton Chandler out of his voice.

Boyd Chandler's eyes narrowed. 'You don't like my son, do you?'

'We . . . don't get on too well,' Danny said, cautiously.

Boyd took a cigar from a wooden box on his desk. He lit it, appraising the young ginger-headed deputy as he did so.

'Guess part of the reason bein' that he won a certain young lady from under your nose. That right?'

Danny made no reply.

Boyd sighed. 'I like you, Danny, but I wouldn't be honest if I didn't admit that I was pleased when Clayton fastened his attentions on the daughter of my best friend, an' then secured her affection. An' I intend to make a handsome contribution towards their future happiness by buildin' a house for them on the Double C.'

Danny sniffed. 'Yeah, well, I can't compete with that, Mr Chandler. But a race ain't over until the horses get to the finishin' line, an' Ellie an' your son ain't married yet.'

Boyd laughed. 'I gotta hand it to you, boy. You don't give up easy, an' I like that in a man. Even so, this is one contest I hope you lose. But listen, if you catch up with Clayton, you might let him have the information you've just given me about the man Hackett.' He stood up and leaned across the desk, offering his hand. 'Best of luck, Danny,' he said.

'Thanks,' Danny said, shaking the older man's hand.

He left soon after, digesting the news about Clayton Chandler's pursuit of the two bank raiders, wondering what it might mean. One thing was for certain. Danny had no intention of sharing any information with Boyd Chandler's son.

He was standing next to his horse,

thinking, when Monte Doyle appeared from behind one of the ranch outbuildings. At first, Danny didn't notice the ranch foreman.

'Hi, Danny,' Monte said. He was in his late thirties, and his questioning grey eyes looked out from under thick eyebrows that almost met in the middle. His face was the colour of old leather. 'You look as though you've got somethin' on your mind.'

He was not a man for small talk, liked to get straight to the point, so Danny obliged him. 'Clayton Chandler.'

Monte sniffed. 'What about him? You lookin' for a character reference for him? 'Cause if'n you are, you've come to the wrong man.'

'He's not like his brother then.'

Monte gave a snort of derision. 'He sure ain't. Scott was a man you could depend on. Honest, hard-workin', never asked you to do anythin' he wouldn't be prepared to do himself. Clayton Chandler? Slippery as a snake. A lazy, double-dealin' critter who drives old man Chandler to despair. Why're you askin' about him?' The corner of Monte's mouth twitched into a brief smile, which vanished almost as soon as it had appeared. ''Cause he stole your girl?'

Danny's face reddened. 'Ellie wasn't my girl.'

'Like her to be though, wouldn't you?' Monte said.

Danny gave a resigned chuckle. 'Is it that obvious?'

'Plain as day to everyone,' Monte said. 'Can't figure why you didn't make your move long ago, afore Clayton Chandler muscled in on the act.'

Danny nodded. 'I should have,' he admitted. 'Wasn't much point once the rich rancher had staked his claim. Couldn't compete.'

'Rich?' Monte said. 'I ain't so sure about that.'

'How d'you mean?' Danny said quickly.

Monte glanced around, then lowered his voice.

'Clayton Chandler likes to play cards.

Poker, mostly. Only he ain't much good at it. Many's the time the hands at the ranch have topped up their pay by winnin' a few dollars off him.'

'That's interestin',' Danny said.

'An' he goes missin' for days at a time.'

'Where's he go?'

'Tucson, mostly. Red Creek a few times. Clyde Morgan who rides shot-gun on the stage has seen him playin' cards with some shifty-lookin' charac-ters in various places. An' you can bet your best saddle he's losin' money most of the time. Or, more'n likely, buildin' up a sizeable marker to some profes-sional gambler or card sharp.'

Or to Wolf Cotton.

The thought sprang into Danny's head. 'Guess Boyd will have to bail him out, if that's the case,' he said, but his thoughts were jumping ahead of his words.

Monte shook his head. 'His pa's had to do it too many times in the past. A few weeks back I heard Boyd give

74

Clayton a final warning about siphonin' off funds from the ranch's bank balance to clear his debts. Nope, Clayton won't have told his pa if he's in a hole. He'll have kept quiet about it. He'll be lookin' for some other way to clear any gamblin' marker somebody's holdin' over him.'

Like using his share in the proceeds from a bank robbery in exchange for supplying a key to the bank.

Danny tried not to show the excitement he was feeling when he asked, 'What was Clayton doin' in town the day of the raid, Monte?'

Monte shrugged. 'Beats me. Said he had some things to pick up from the store, but it's more likely he had some card-playin' pals to meet in the saloon.'

Danny thought back. Clayton Chandler had emerged from the saloon after the shooting had stopped, it was true.

'Gotta go, Monte,' he said.

Monte looked at him and closed one eye in a slow wink. 'Be a good time to go callin' on a young lady, seein' as the competition's gone a-huntin'.'

Danny grinned. 'I'll be seein' you,' he said.

★ ★ ★

By this time, Clayton was well on his way to Red Creek, having been to see Ellie before leaving Suta Springs. Her mother had taken to her bed, still unable to grasp what had happened, and Ellie had seemed to have taken charge of things. She had been sorting through her father's papers at a roll-top desk in the study. She took Clayton into the parlour and they sat next to one another on a window seat overlooking the garden.

'It's good to see you Clayton,' she said. 'How's your father?'

'He's grievin' real bad,' Clayton said. 'I suggested that I went after Julie's murderer, an' Pa agreed. Pa would go himself, but he don't want to leave Ma, her bein' the way she is.' Clayton took her hand in his. 'Also, I owe it to you

76

an' your pa to find his killer, Ellie.'

'Oh, Clayton, are you sure about this?' Ellie's eyes took on a worried expression. 'Pa wouldn't want you to put yourself in danger and — and nor do I.'

Clayton lifted her hand to his lips and kissed it. 'Don't you go worryin' about me. I can take good care of myself.'

Now, heading west on the trail to Red Creek, he felt nothing like as confident. The thought of maybe having to kill Curtis Jordan made him feel physically sick with fear. Jordan was an experienced gunman. Many men had tried to kill him in the past and died for their pains.

But the real problem was Danny Ridge. If the young deputy should get to Jordan or Drew Hudson before Clayton, then Clayton's part in the raid would almost certainly come out.

Which ever way you dealt the cards, killing Ridge seemed the best and safest bet.

9

Curtis Jordan was enjoying the diversions of one Sadie Partridge, a busty brunette who had known a few tricks that even Curtis hadn't come across before.

Finally, as he rolled off the bed and began pulling on his pants he turned back to Sadie.

'The barkeep reckons Drew Hudson's left town,' he said. 'You know anythin' about that?'

Sadie shrugged, stretching her naked body under the bedcovers. 'Well now . . . maybe,' she said, slyly.

But her mischievous smile froze when she saw Curtis's steely-eyed reaction. He yanked the bedcovers off her, pulled her from the bed and on to the floor, then twisted her wrist until the pain turned her whole arm numb.

'Don't mess me about, Sadie,' he

said, coldly. 'You got anythin' to say, then say it!'

'OK, OK!' she gasped. 'Please! You're hurtin' me.' He slackened his grip fractionally but held on. 'I ain't sure about it, but Drew used to talk about an aunt of theirs in Latimer. His sister was always pesterin' him to agree to movin' there. Could be they've gone there, but Herbie Calhoun would know for sure.'

'He would, would he?' Curtis said, releasing Sadie's arm. 'Now that's interestin'. The double-dealin' bastard reckoned he knew nothin'.'

He pushed Sadie's naked body away from him and finished dressing. 'Guess I need to pay your storekeeper another visit,' he said. 'But first I need a drink.'

★   ★   ★

Polecat watched as Curtis emerged from Sadie's room and made his way downstairs.

'Quite a girl, Sadie, ain't she?' Polecat

remarked, when the other man reached the bar. He pushed a glass and a bottle of red-eye towards him.

Curtis poured himself a drink without answering.

Polecat lowered his voice. 'Fella came in last night, from outa town. Said somethin' about a bank raid in Suta Springs.'

'Yeah?' Curtis swallowed his drink, suddenly wary. He looked closely at Polecat. From the knowing look on the other man's face, one thing seemed certain. The barkeep had somehow made a connection between Curtis and the bank raid.

But Curtis had the feeling that Polecat wasn't the sort to go running to the sheriff with this information, not if it could be turned to his advantage. Which almost certainly meant blackmail. What Polecat wouldn't know, was that Curtis didn't have any of the bank's money, and would be in no position to pay him to keep his mouth shut.

The touch wasn't long in coming.

'They reckon it were the Cotton gang who pulled the job,' Polecat went on. 'Two of 'em were killed, but two of 'em got away. My guess is, Drew Hudson was one of the critters who escaped.' He dropped his voice to almost a whisper and leaned closer to Curtis. 'And I reckon you, *Mister Jordan*, were the other.'

Curtis was equally soft-voiced in his reply. 'You call me by that name again, friend, an' you'll be dead meat.'

Polecat sniffed. ''Course, if'n the law comes askin' around — well, seems to me I oughta get some sorta *compensation* for bein' discreet. What d'you reckon, *Mister Smith*?'

Curtis poured himself another drink and downed it in one. 'We'll talk about that later,' he said. Then he turned and walked out of the saloon.

'We sure will,' Polecat said, watching him.

* * *

Herbie Calhoun's stomach somersaulted when Curtis Jordan entered the store. Curtis shut and locked the store door and pulled down the blind. The smile he gave Herbie was like a rabid coyote showing its teeth before an attack.

'Seems you weren't completely honest with me, mister storekeeper,' he growled.

'I — that's not true, I — that is . . . ' Herbie felt his bowels loosening as Curtis drew one of his Colts.

'Latimer,' Curtis said. 'That's where the Hudson pair've gone, ain't it?'

'Maybe,' Herbie admitted. 'I'd forgotten — '

'No, you hadn't!' Curtis snarled. 'You lied! Hudson an' his sister have gone to Latimer. Ain't that right?'

'I-I don't know, truly I don't. Sure, it's possible, but I can't be certain.'

'Tell me about their aunt,' Curtis demanded. 'What's her name?'

'Bella Gower,' Herbie said. 'She runs a café in Latimer. Honest, mister, that's all I know.'

The gunslinger snatched a pair of overalls from one of the stands of clothes and balled them up in his hand. He held them in front of the Colt's barrel.

'No, please!' Herbie pleaded.

The overalls muffled the sound of the shot, but a crimson stain appeared on the storekeeper's chest as he crashed back into the shelving behind him. The shelves collapsed and their contents toppled to the floor around him. Curtis's second bullet made a hole dead centre in Herbie's forehead. Herbie's unblinking eyes stared at the ceiling.

Curtis dropped the overalls on the floor and went round the other side of the counter. He opened the cash drawer and helped himself to the paper money inside it, then he walked through to the back room and went out through the rear door into an alleyway. He looked up and down and, satisfied nobody had heard the gunshots and had come running, moved out into the main street.

'Next stop, Latimer,' Curtis said to

himself. 'But I've a little business to attend to first.'

★ ★ ★

Shortly after midnight, Polecat came out into the alleyway at the rear of the Green Garter. He was carrying a crate of empty bottles, ready to stack it on the waist-high heap of crates by the back doors. It was dark in the alleyway, and it stank where patrons of the saloon often relieved themselves of their alcoholic intake. Having deposited the crate on the pile, Polecat half-turned to go back into the building when he heard movement and saw a shadowy figure materialize from the darkness.

Too late, he saw the glint of the knife blade before the weapon was plunged into his throat. Polecat made a horrible gurgling sound and staggered backwards. Twice more the knife sank into his neck before Curtis Jordan wiped the blade clean on Polecat's pants, then sheathed the knife in his boot.

After checking that Main Street was clear, Curtis picked up his saddle-bags from the corner where he'd left them, then emerged from the alleyway and walked towards the hitching rail where he'd left his horse. He climbed aboard the animal.

'Latimer, here I come,' he muttered.

10

At the same time as Curtis Jordan rode away from Red Creek, across the street at the Cornstalk Hotel, Clayton Chandler slept heavily after his long and tiring ride from the Double C ranch. He had arrived an hour earlier and, after checking with the hotel clerk that nobody of Curtis Jordan's description was staying there, had taken a room and collapsed on to the bed.

Next morning he went down to breakfast where another guest, a none-too-prosperous-looking drummer in a frayed blue suit, sat at a table opposite him. They were the only two occupants of the dining room. The Cornstalk was a run-down, slightly seedy establishment, but the food was passable and Clayton's bed had been clean if board-hard.

'Name's Pike,' the drummer said,

smiling at Clayton. 'Wilf Pike.' He was a skinny little guy with a drooping moustache. He wore narrow eyeglasses and the sun, coming through the dust-streaked windows, shone on the lenses directly, turning them into blank mirrors which concealed his eyes.

Clayton found it disconcerting. He nodded at him but said nothing.

'Just passing through like me?' the little man asked.

'Maybe,' Clayton said.

He attacked his ham and eggs, not wishing to engage in conversation. A passing-through drummer would be unlikely to be of use to him, he decided.

He was wrong.

'Hear about the two killings last night?' the drummer said.

Clayton gave him a quizzical look. 'What's that?'

'Got it from the clerk in the lobby. He heard it from some delivery man.'

'Who got killed?' Clayton asked.

'Barkeep at the Green Garter. Pole-cat, his name was.' The drummer used his finger and thumb to smooth down the ends of his moustache. 'Well, that's what everybody called him. Big guy, apparently. Not an easy man to kill, accordin' to the clerk here. Other victim was the owner of the local mercantile.'

'How'd they die?' Clayton asked.

'Barkeep was stabbed to death in the alleyway at the back of the saloon,' the little man told him. 'Storekeeper was shot in his store.'

'Do they know who did it?'

'Nope. Reckon it was the same man though.'

Curtis Jordan?

Clayton suddenly lost interest in his ham and eggs, his appetite gone. He drank the last dregs of his coffee and got up.

'Take care now,' the drummer said as Clayton went past the little man.

'I intend to,' Clayton said to himself as he passed through the dining room doorway and into the lobby.

The hotel clerk was a different man from the one he'd seen the night before. Even so, this clerk also assured Clayton that no one of Curtis Jordan's description was amongst the guests.

'Besides you and the drummer,' he said, 'there's only an elderly married couple staying in the hotel.'

'What do you know about a man named Drew Hudson?' Clayton asked.

The clerk frowned and thought for a moment. 'I vaguely remember him. Not that he ate in the hotel very often.' He gave a knowing smile. 'I think the — er — attractions of the Green Garter were more persuasive.'

'Attractions?'

'Mm. Particularly a Miss Sadie Partridge, I'm told. However, I think you'll find Mr Hudson has left town, but Sadie will probably know more about that.'

Clayton went outside. There were very few people in the street, and those who were were huddled together in deep discussion, probably talking about the two murders.

The bright sun threw deep shadows

across the boardwalks opposite and, although still early in the day, the heat hit Clayton like a fiery fist as he crossed the street to the Green Garter.

The dead barkeep had been replaced by a wispy-bearded older man with wire-rimmed spectacles.

'What can I get you?' he asked Clayton.

'You can tell me where to find Sadie Partridge,' Clayton told him.

The barkeep raised his eyes towards the top of the stairs. 'Third room on the right,' he said.

Clayton turned and headed for the stairs.

11

In Latimer, Drew Hudson was pacing up and down a hotel room.

'I ain't so sure this is a good idea,' he said. 'Comin' to a place where we've got relations.'

'One relation,' Kate corrected him. 'Aunt Bella. Besides, it was your suggestion.'

'Yeah, I know, but now I ain't so sure.'

'And you were concerned about getting further away from Suta Springs. Well, Latimer's fifty miles or more from there and seventy miles from Red Creek.'

They were both irritable and exhausted after two days of travelling. Drew had persuaded Kate to let him book rooms at the Prime Hotel, using some of the money from the bank raid.

'We can afford it now,' he had told her.

Drew had given her an edited version of the events in Suta Springs. As far as Kate knew, there had been no killing of innocent people (Drew had not mentioned his shooting of the bank manager), only the three members of the Cotton gang. In truth, Drew couldn't be certain of Curtis Jordan's death, but he wasn't going to tell Kate that. The last he'd seen of Curtis, the raider's horse had been brought down but whether or not Curtis himself had been killed, Drew couldn't be sure. And then there was the other *hombre*, the one who'd got Wolf a duplicate key for the bank's back door. *He* wasn't dead, and he might come looking for Drew, expecting a cut of the money.

Which was the chief reason he was unhappy about their presence in a town which had family connections. It could be a lead for Curtis or the other man to follow up if they were looking for him. Which Curtis surely would be if he was alive. Why hadn't he thought of this earlier, damn it?

'You ever mentioned Aunt Bella to anyone in Red Creek?' he asked Kate now. He was trying to remember if he'd ever mentioned their relation to Sadie at the Green Garter. He had a horrible feeling he had. Would the little whore keep her mouth shut, if that was the case?

Kate answered cautiously 'I-I don't think so.'

'You sure?'

'Yes. Why are you so worried, Drew? You said that nobody could have identified you after the robbery; that you were masked.'

'I was.'

'And that the other three members of the gang were killed.'

'Yeah, well, they were.'

'Then I don't understand why you're worried. Nobody who saw the robbery knows your face. And no posse is going to spend days trying to find a trail which you say you covered.'

'I guess it's — it's just that me an' Aunt Bella never did get on.' It was a weak response and he knew it.

'Things can change,' Kate told him. 'Besides, she may be able to help me find work. Maybe I can wait tables in her café. I've waited tables before. Or I could get work clerking or as a seamstress. Aunt Bella will know what work opportunities there are here.'

'But that's just it,' Drew said. 'You don't *need* to work now.'

'I have to earn money,' she said.

'We've got money, Kate!' Drew said, irritated by her stubbornness. 'We can buy a house or — or live in the best rooms in this hotel. We can — '

'No!' she snapped. 'It's dirty money. I don't want any of it!'

'That's crazy!' he said, anger swelling up inside him. 'Eleven thousand dollars! More money than we've ever seen. Well, I sure as hell am goin' to use it.'

'How?' she said. 'Gambling? Whoring?'

He was infuriated by her attitude but tried to control his temper. 'I-I could start a business. Maybe a mercantile, like old man Calhoun.'

'You're dreaming, Drew. You've about as much business sense as a coyote.'

'OK, so I could learn!'

Kate sighed. 'I'm through arguing. I'm dog-tired.'

'Sure, sure,' he said, taking a conciliatory tone. 'We're both tired. We'll talk about this in the morning. Get some sleep.'

He left her and went to his room along the passage. Once inside he threw himself fully clothed on the bed and stared at the ceiling. Suddenly, the elation of getting away with all that money had drained away. His mood had soured after his argument with Kate. He was angry and exasperated with her. Hell, she should have been excited about having all that money. Should've been dazzled by his daring, hooking up with one of the most famous gangs in this part of the West. It hadn't been easy, persuading Wolf Cotton to take him in. Left to Ab Cooper and Curtis Jordan, he'd still be bumming drinks in the Green Garter and cheating at cards to

95

make a few bucks. Luckily, he apparently bore a striking resemblance to the dead Virgil Cotton, and that had swung it. That plus the fact that Wolf Cotton had always liked to have a gang of four. It was his lucky number, he'd told Drew.

Drew smiled. Well, it had been lucky for him. Eleven thousand dollars lucky!

★　★　★

In her own room, Kate was also stretched out on her bed. But tired as she was, sleep refused to come. Her mind was a maelstrom of thoughts. How much of Drew's story about the bank robbery was true? Had no innocent person really not been hurt? And why was he looking over his shoulder all the time if what he had said about the other three gangsters being killed was true? And how much was she going to tell Aunt Bella about their sudden departure from Red Creek and their arrival in Latimer? Aunt Bella was no fool. She would know that something was wrong.

Kate thought about Mr Calhoun. What did the poor man think about them now, after they'd stolen his buckboard and fled? She was attacked with a pang of guilt. She had mentioned Aunt Bella to Mr Calhoun once or twice, but she had no intention of telling Drew this. For some reason she didn't understand, it would probably be enough for him to force them to leave town.

'And this time we're staying!' Kate said aloud to herself.

12

'You want a little entertainin', mister?' Sadie asked, adopting a well-rehearsed coyness in her voice and demeanour. She sat in the centre of the large bed, her knees drawn up to her chin. The only thing she was wearing was her smile.

Clayton swallowed. 'Maybe later,' he said.

Sadie feigned disappointment. 'That's too bad. What can I do for you then?'

'Information about a man called Drew Hudson.'

'You too?' Sadie said, before she stopped to think. Then she swore silently to herself.

'Somebody else been askin' about him?' Clayton said.

Sadie shook her head. 'No, I got it wrong, mister. I — '

Clayton was across the room in a

flash. He pushed her down flat on to the bed and held a hand around her neck.

'Who else was askin'?' he demanded. 'What was his name?'

'I don't know!' Sadie whined. 'I didn't ask. I *never* ask.'

'Describe him.' Clayton raised his hand, as if about to strike her.

Sadie shrieked, but then gave an accurate description of Curtis Jordan.

'What did you tell him?' Clayton asked.

'That Drew Hudson an' his sister've probably gone to Latimer,' Sadie admitted. 'They've got an aunt there who runs a café. I don't know her name.'

Clayton took his hand away from her neck. He smiled slowly and began to unbutton his pants.

'Now you can do a little entertainin',' he said.

★ ★ ★

When Danny arrived in Red Creek, he went straight to the building at the end of the main street: the one with the words *Walt Hatch, Liveryman* over the doorway.

The grizzled old-timer who greeted him gave Danny a toothless smile.

'Howdy, son,' Walt said. 'What can I do fer you?'

'Apart from 'tending my horse, you can tell me where I can find the owner of that fine animal in the far stall,' Danny said. He'd noticed it the minute he'd come in, unable to believe his good luck. 'The one with the white markin's.'

'That's me,' Walt said. 'You interested in buyin' her?'

'Nope,' Danny said. 'But I guess you bought her just recently. In the last coupla days, in fact.'

'Now how'd you know that?' Walt asked, brows furrowed. He hawked and spat. 'Were you a friend of Drew's?'

'Drew?' Danny said. 'Drew who?'

'Drew Hudson,' Walt told him. 'Used to live at the mercantile with his sister.

Kate's a nice girl. Always made time for a chat whenever I went into the store. They've got an aunt in Latimer, she told me once. Most likely that's where they've gone. Left town in a kinda hurry, a day or so ago. Now folks are askin' if Drew's high-tailin' it has anythin' to do with Herbie Calhoun's murder. Herbie was the owner of the mercantile.'

'Murder?' Danny perched himself on the edge of a bale of straw. 'Reckon you'd better tell me some more, Walt.' And he took his deputy's badge from his waistcoat pocket for the old man to scrutinize.

Walt stared at it. 'Reckon I had,' he said, after a moment.

★   ★   ★

Clayton was fully dressed and had a satisfied smirk on his face. He peeled two one-dollar bills from a roll and dropped them on top of the washstand in Sadie's room.

'That should cover it,' he said. 'An' speakin' of 'coverin' it' . . . ' He yanked the bed sheet over Sadie's naked form. 'Put the goods away ready for the next customer, Sadie!'

He laughed loudly and walked from the room.

Sadie gave a sigh. 'Thank goodness for that!' she thought. 'But why all this interest in Drew Hudson suddenly? The little squirt was nothing special in bed, that's for sure!'

Clayton emerged from the Green Garter, intending to go back to the hotel and check out before starting on the long journey to Latimer. But the sight of Danny Ridge talking with the livery-man at the end of the street stopped him in his tracks.

So the meddling young deputy had somehow connected Red Creek with one or both of the bank raiders. How in hell had he done that so *fast*? Clayton had reckoned on at least a few more days before having to worry about Danny Ridge.

Question was, should he confront him and find out what he knew, or stay out of his way? Clayton decided on the latter. It was unlikely Ridge would have anything useful to add to what Clayton had already discovered. It was more important to put a stop to the deputy's manhunt as soon as possible.

'Maybe tonight, under cover of darkness,' he thought.

Using backstreets, he made his way to the hotel and slipped in through a kitchen door. He threaded his way through into the lobby and accosted the hotel clerk again.

'Any new guests?' Clayton asked.

'No, sir,' came the reply.

'How far is it to Latimer?'

'Latimer? About seventy miles,' the man replied.

'Make up my bill. I'll be checking out later.' Clayton said, and retreated to his room.

★ ★ ★

Twenty minutes later, Danny checked into the Cornstalk.

'Just the one night,' he told the clerk. 'I'll be leavin' for Latimer tomorrow.'

The clerk blinked. 'Suddenly a very popular place, it seems.'

Danny became instantly alert. 'Oh, why?'

'Gentleman was asking how far away it was only a few minutes ago.'

'What gentleman?' Danny asked. And when the clerk seemed reluctant to tell him, flashed his deputy's star.

The clerk checked the hotel register. 'A Mr Chandler,' he informed Danny.

Danny smiled. 'That so? He stayin' here?'

The clerk nodded.

'And he's plannin' a trip to Latimer in the near future,' Danny said. 'Hm. Well, I guess I'll just rest up for a couple of hours, then I'll check out what Red Creek has to offer. Maybe I'll bump into Mr Chandler.'

The clerk watched him head for the stairs and wondered if he should say something about Mr Chandler's seemingly imminent departure from the hotel. In the end, he decided against it. Guests at the Cornstalk deserved a little privacy, he told himself.

13

Ten minutes before eleven Danny emerged from the Green Garter saloon and made his way back towards the Cornstalk, using the boardwalk. He was slightly disappointed that he hadn't run into Clayton Chandler all evening, in spite of visiting various places of entertainment. But he planned to be down to the hotel dining room first thing the next morning, ready to greet his rival for Ellie's affections, and maybe surprise him.

What he didn't know was that, although he'd seen nothing of Clayton, the latter had been keeping an eye on Danny from a safe distance ever since the young deputy had left the hotel after his siesta.

Now, sitting in a high-back chair and hidden in the shadows of the boardwalk across the street, Clayton watched him heading for the hotel.

Clayton glanced around, but the street was deserted. He stood up, removed his six-gun from its holster, and took a bead on the other man. Sweat broke out on his head and he had trouble holding his gun steady.

Holding his breath, he waited until Danny moved a little ahead of him . . . then shot the young deputy in the back.

Clayton watched Danny fall to the ground, then he scuttled down a side-street, along the backs of the buildings on Main Street until he was able to cross over and make his way back to the Cornstalk without drawing attention to himself.

By this time, Danny's body was surrounded by a handful of people, including the hotel clerk.

Clayton slipped into the Cornstalk. He'd left his bag with the clerk earlier, and was able to collect it from the little office behind the hotel desk without anyone seeing him.

Earlier he had decided that, even with Danny Ridge dead, his complicity in the Suta Springs bank raid could never be certain to remain a secret as long as Drew Hudson and Curtis Jordan were alive. He had to follow through and eliminate both of them, even though the mere thought of it made him sick to the stomach.

Once outside the hotel, keeping to the shadows, he made his way to the livery. In passing, he saw that Danny's body was being carried to a house near the hotel. The undertaker's? Danny didn't wait to enquire. However, he noted that the old-timer from the livery was one of a huddle of people still out on the street debating what had happened. Another was the local sheriff. No doubt the livery man was telling the lawman about his earlier encounter with Danny.

Clayton quietly removed his horse from the livery by way of the back doors of the stable. He was startled to see Drew Hudson's black stallion in one of the stalls. Could he have got it wrong? Was Drew holed up somewhere in town? But, after a moment's thought, Clayton reasoned that Drew had probably sold the horse because of the animal's distinctive markings.

He walked his own horse through the backstreets until he reached the edge of the town, and only then did he mount the animal and spur it into action.

As he did so, lightning spider-webbed across the night sky, followed seconds later by the drumroll of thunder. Large splats of rain began to fall.

Clayton grinned. 'Nice heavy storm'll cover my tracks,' he muttered. 'Even the rain's on my side.' And he began to laugh loudly.

★   ★   ★

The house near the Green Garter where the little band of people had gently carried Danny was not, as Clayton had supposed, the undertaker's. It was Doc Kelly's home and surgery.

109

'You were lucky,' Doc Kelly told Danny. 'I think I can get the slug out without touching your spine. It's gonna hurt like hell, but you'll live.'

Danny, lying face down on the medical man's scrubbed pine kitchen table, shirt cut open down the back, gave an almost imperceptible nod. His face was creased with pain. He could hear the sound of heavy rain outside, and the rumble of thunder.

'I'm going to give you some laudanum,' Doc Kelly went on. 'When it starts to work, so will I.'

Two hours later, Danny was sleeping off the effects of the laudanum in the doc's spare room, the bullet safely removed from his back. It had been easier to get at than the doc had feared.

Doc Kelly was talking to the sheriff downstairs.

'So who is he, Hank? Do you have any idea?'

Sheriff Hank McGee nodded. 'Been talkin' to Walt Hatch at the livery. Apparently your patient is a man called

Ridge. Totes a deputy's badge, too.'

'Think he's chasing the man who killed Herbie and Polecat?'

'He was askin' Walt about Drew Hudson.'

'Hudson?' Doc Kelly said. 'That good-for-nothing? Why would he want to know about him?'

'Can't tell you,' McGee answered. 'Anyway, come daylight, I'll get a posse together an' we'll try an' find his shooter's trail.' He grimaced as another crash of thunder rumbled away in the distance. 'Although I doubt there'll be anythin' to find after that storm.'

'What's happening in this town, Hank?' Doc said. 'Two murders and an attempted murder all in the space of twenty-four hours? The three incidents have got to be connected. Maybe the link is Drew Hudson.'

'But what's so special about Hudson?'

'Don't know, but he left town in a hurry, didn't he?' Doc said.

'True,' the sheriff agreed. He looked out of the window where pale streaks of light were beginning to stain the night sky. 'Anyway, I'd best be gettin' that posse together. It'll be daylight soon.'

Three hours later, an exasperated Sheriff McGee and a dispirited group of men returned to Red Creek, having given up any hope of finding a trail.

14

'My God, girl, you've lost some weight since I last saw you!' Bella Gower looked her niece up and down. 'What in tarnation have you been doin'?'

They were in Bella's café — The Eating House — in Latimer's Main Street. It was mid-morning, a quiet time before the lunchtime eaters descended on the place demanding food.

Kate gave a shaky smile and planted a kiss on her aunt's cheek. 'I'm fine, Aunt Bella.'

Bella Gower's eyes narrowed. 'So what you doin' here? Not that I ain't pleased to see you, you understand. Told you to come often enough. But how'd you get here? Stage?'

'N-o,' Kate said slowly. 'We — we came by buckboard.'

'"We"?' Bella's face fell. 'You tellin' me you got that no-good brother of yours with you?'

'Now, Aunt, *please*,' Kate said. 'I know you don't think much of Drew, but — '

'You're right, I don't,' Bella cut in. 'Trouble with a capital T, always has been. Young hellion ain't worth spit!' She looked over Kate's shoulder. 'Anyway, what've you done with him?'

'He — he's at the hotel,' Kate said. It was just possible, she thought, although more likely that he'd found his way to one of the saloons, straining at the leash to lose some of his ill-gotten money at poker. But she wasn't going to tell her aunt that.

'Stayin' at the hotel, are you?' Bella said, a suspicious look in her eye. She was a big woman, and folded her arms across her ample stomach. 'You come into money, or somethin'?'

'Drew got a lucky streak,' Kate replied. 'He's a sort of professional gambler, these days, Aunt.'

It was the story she and Drew had decided on before she'd left the hotel earlier that morning. But she could already see the scepticism in her aunt's eyes.

'He is, is he?' Bella said. She sniffed, dismissing the idea as less than important. 'Main thing is, you've come, an' lookin' pretty as a picture, as usual, even if you are a bit on the skinny side. I'll have to fatten you up!'

Kate laughed, relieved that her aunt seemed to have accepted the situation. 'I was hoping you could find me some work. I don't mind waiting tables. Or maybe I could help out in the kitchen.'

'Let's not worry about that today. Maybe tomorrow, or the day after. I'm just goin' to enjoy havin' you around me for a time. You still keepin' up with your drawin'? Always reckoned you could make a little money from that.'

'I still draw, yes, Aunt,' Kate conceded. 'But it's just a hobby. I'm no artist.'

'You eaten today?' Bella asked.

Kate nodded. 'Had breakfast at the hotel.'

'Huh! Hotel food! Listen, why don't you leave that brother of yours there an' come an' stay with me. I've got plenty of room, spinster-lady like I am.' She chuckled. 'Your mother never stopped tryin' to find me a man, mind you. Lost cause, I used to tell her, but she wouldn't have it, God rest her soul.'

'I-I guess I *could* come and stay,' Kate said. She knew that Drew wouldn't care; would probably be relieved not to have her checking up on him all the time.

''Course you could,' her aunt said. 'I'll get your room ready for you pronto! You go back to the hotel and get your things.' She gave her niece a hug. 'Your comin' is the nicest thing that's happened to me in a long time. I'm gonna cook something special for us. Put some meat on that skinny frame of yours!'

Kate laughed. 'OK,' she said, thankful that the older woman hadn't asked about the nature of their departure from Red Creek. Whether it had been a leisurely one or whether they'd spent most of the journey looking over their shoulders. Which they had.

15

In Red Creek, Danny woke to see sunlight streaming through the bedroom window. For some moments he could not remember where he was, then it all came flooding back. He pushed down the bed covers and saw the broad bandage that went around his chest and back. A dull, throbbing came from the place where Doc Kelly had removed the bullet.

'So, you're awake.' Doc Kelly's voice came from the doorway. He was holding a pot of coffee and two mugs.

Danny eased himself up on to his elbows, only to discover that he was as weak as a new-born calf.

Doc chuckled. 'Yes, well it's going to be a day or two before you'll be on your feet. Here, have some coffee. I'll get you something to eat later.'

He put the mugs on the table next to

the bed and began pouring out the hot liquid.

'Need to be gone sooner than that,' Danny said.

'Gone where?' Doc asked.

'Latimer,' Danny told him.

'That's more than seventy miles away. What's waiting for you in Latimer?'

'The man who shot me, I reckon. 'Cept he won't be waitin' around, not once he's attended to his business.'

'And what's that?'

'Depends on who he is. Could be one of two fellas. If it's a man called Clayton Chandler, he *could*'ve returned to Suta Springs. But my guess is he'll want to find Curtis Jordan and Drew Hudson. If it's Curtis Jordan, he'll be wantin' to find and kill Hudson,' Danny said. He sipped the scalding coffee. 'But only after he's got his share of the money.'

'Money?'

'From the Suta Springs bank raid,' Danny said.

Doc's eyebrows shot up. 'Drew Hudson

was involved in a *bank robbery*? I can't believe it.'

'Well, I'm pretty sure it's true.'

Doc gave him an enquiring look. 'You a lawman? Sheriff McGee reckons you are.'

Danny nodded.

'You won't be fit to ride for at least a week,' Doc said.

'I can't give my shooter that much time,' Danny said. 'An' once he leaves Latimer, his trail will go cold.'

Doc sighed. 'Well, there's a stage to Latimer,' he said. 'Due here day after tomorrow. I guess that'd be kinder on your injuries than riding a horse.'

'Then I'll take the stage. Guess it'll be OK to leave my horse in the livery an' come back for it later.'

'Sure,' Doc said. 'Walt will look after your animal.'

'Thanks,' Scott said. Then added, 'For everthin'.'

Doc smiled. 'My pleasure,' he said.

16

Drew rolled off the voluptuous body of Lottie Parks, every man's favourite at Opal's House — Opal Harris's saloon and whorehouse in Latimer's red-light district.

He gasped with exhaustion as the bed creaked under him. 'Jeeze, Lottie, you sure know how to pleasure a man!'

Lottie, a redhead with breasts the size of ripe honeydew melons, gave a throaty chuckle. 'Why thank you, sir. I aim to please.'

Drew had availed himself of Lottie's services each evening for the past few days before returning to his room at the hotel. By day he hung out at one or other of Latimer's three saloons, playing poker or faro and — if truth were told — losing more of his money each time.

He drank a lot, too. This helped to

suppress the anger he felt at Kate's refusal to have anything to do with the money, her departure from her room at the hotel and her taking up residence at Bella Gower's café.

Drew pulled on his clothes.

'You goin', kid?' Lottie asked.

'Don't call me kid!' Drew snapped. He stalked across to the window and looked down into the darkening street below. A few lamps had come on in some of the other buildings, mostly whorehouses and bars.

Lottie winced at his strident tone. She had a feeling this kid — she still thought of him as little more than a kid — could be dangerous if made mad enough, and she didn't aim to find out.

'You're right,' she said, soothingly. 'You sure ain't no kid in bed, Drew. You're plumb manly the way you . . . well, you know.'

Drew grinned. 'Just you remember that, an' — ' He stopped suddenly and the blood drained from his face.

'Somethin' wrong?' Lottie said. 'You

121

seen somethin'?'

Drew didn't answer. He was watching the man tying his horse to the hitch rail outside the Bib'n Tucker Bar opposite. At first, he hadn't been sure, but as soon as the man moved into the light that was spilling out over the batwings of the bar, there was no mistaking the face of Curtis Jordan.

Lottie wrapped a sheet around herself and padded across the room to join Drew at the window. She followed the direction of his gaze, then said, 'You know that man?'

'Yeah, I know him,' Drew said, after a moment. His heart was thumping in his chest.

'He come lookin' for you?' Lottie asked.

Drew nodded. 'I reckon.'

'But you ain't pleased to see him.'

'You can say that again.' He moved away from the window as Curtis Jordan disappeared into the bar. 'I gotta get out of here, Lottie. Out of Latimer.'

Lottie stared at him. 'That bad?' she

said. 'What you done to him, honey?'

'I've got somethin' he wants,' Drew said.

'So give it to him.'

'It ain't that simple.'

Drew strapped on his gunbelt. He needed to get back to the hotel fast to remove his things and check out before Curtis thought to find out whether or not he was staying there.

He left Lottie still wrapped in the sheet, hurried out of the room and down the stairs. Even as he half-ran, he tried to gather his thoughts.

'Quit panickin',' he told himself. 'Think!'

There was little more than half the bank money left now, but half would be a fair share for Curtis. What he would've expected to get. Of course, it would leave him, Drew, with nothing, but maybe Curtis would overlook his running away if he got his share of the loot.

'Who am I kiddin'?' Drew said to himself as he ran along the street, keeping to the shadows and casting frequent glances over his shoulder. 'He's gonna kill me. Jeeze, I wish I'd never set eyes on Wolf Cotton. Never got involved in his damned bank raid! If only I could turn the clock back!'

On the other hand, Curtis wasn't likely to shoot him on sight or there would be no way of finding what was left of the money. Also he, Drew, could not spend the rest of his life running from Curtis.

So there had to be another answer. The thing was to stay out of the other man's way for as long as possible, and make a plan. A plan which might *not* mean leaving town.

'Maybe now would be a good time to make amends with Aunt Bella and move in there, at least for the time bein',' he muttered to himself.

The hotel clerk at the Prime Hotel was reading the local newspaper but looked up when Drew came in.

'Anybody been in askin' for me?' Drew wanted to know.

The clerk shook his head. 'No, sir.'

'Good,' Drew said. 'I'll be checkin' out.'

'Oh?' the clerk said.

'Yeah, have my bill ready by the time I come down.'

★　★　★

Opal Harris had watched Drew's hasty departure from her establishment with interest. She had been in the business long enough to tell the difference between a man who had to scuttle because his wife was coming looking for him, and one who feared for his life.

Opal dragged her eighteen-and-half stone of flesh and fat up the stairs to Lottie Parks' room and pushed open the door without knocking.

Lottie, clad only in her chemise, was sitting on the edge of her bed, looking thoughtful. She glanced up, unsurprised, as Opal entered.

'Left in kind of a hurry, your client, Lottie,' Opal said. 'Somethin' wrong?'

Lottie assumed an innocent expression and shrugged.

'Don't know.'

Opal stepped forward and slapped her hard across the face. 'Don't lie to me, girl! He was outa here faster'n a jack rabbit. Scared half to death, too. What happened?'

Lottie rubbed her stinging face. 'Honest, Opal, he didn't say,' she whined. 'He looked out of the window, saw somethin' an' ran.'

'Didn't you look outa the window?'

'Sure, but I didn't see anythin'. Maybe he saw that sister of his an' didn't want to be caught in a whorehouse.'

'Horseshit!' Opal snapped. 'She wouldn't put a step in a place like this even if'n she did know her brother was pleasurin' himself with a whore. Which, mostly, I reckon she does know. From what I've seen of her, the lady ain't no fool. Nope, it was somethin' else.' Opal's eyes narrowed in thought. 'Reckon he saw someone he didn't want to see,' she said eventually. 'Some mystery man.

126

Wonder who it was?'

If she could find out, there would be one of two ways of making a bit of extra money. Either by getting the mystery man to pay for information about Drew Hudson, or from Drew for keeping her mouth shut. First, though, she needed to discover the identity of the critter who was scaring the pants off Drew Hudson.

'If'n Drew comes back, see what you can find out,' she told Lottie.

'Sure, Opal,' Lottie answered.

Opal left, slamming the door behind her.

Lottie smiled, pleased with herself. She liked Drew and had no intention of helping Opal to put the screws on him. In fact, if there was anything she could do to help the kid, then she'd do it. Although he'd said he was leaving town.

17

Drew headed for Bella Gower's eating house via Latimer's backstreets, carpet-bag in hand. The loot from the bank was in a money belt which he'd bought from the mercantile a few days earlier. The belt was under his shirt. It had been a secure enough place until Curtis Jordan's arrival, but now it felt vulner-able. He needed to find somewhere safer.

The café was closed, it being nearly ten o'clock, so Drew went round to the rear door. There was a light in the back room, and there was a crack between the drawn curtains through which he could see his aunt and sister sitting either side of a pot-bellied stove. Bella was slumped in her chair dozing, whilst Kate had her sketchbook in front of her and was working with a pencil. She appeared to be making a drawing of her sleeping aunt. Drew smiled to himself as he watched her.

Preferring not to wake his aunt if he could help it, he tapped on the window. Startled, Kate looked up, put down her sketchbook and pencil then came across. She eased back one of the curtains and looked out, her face registering surprise and alarm when she recognized her brother.

Drew put a finger to his lips, then pointed to the back door. Understanding the silent message, Kate let the curtain drop. Seconds later, she opened the door. She immediately saw the carpetbag Drew was carrying and frowned.

'What's wrong?' she whispered, after glancing back at her sleeping aunt.

'Nothin',' Drew replied, keeping his voice low. 'I just thought I'd come an' stay here. Got tired of stayin' at the hotel.'

'I'm not sure Aunt Bella will welcome you,' she told him.

'Aw, Kate, you can fix it. She'll listen to you.'

'There's no place for you to sleep,'

she said. 'I've got the only spare room, and it's only got the one bed.'

'I can sleep in there, on the couch.' He pointed behind her. 'Come on, Kate. Let me in.'

Reluctantly, Kate moved back and opened the door so that he could enter.

Bella Gower chose that exact moment to wake up. She blinked rapidly, taking in Drew's presence in the room with a quickening of her breath.

Drew smiled at her. 'Howdy, Aunt Bella.'

Aunt Bella sighed. 'Why do I get the feelin' our peace has ended, Kate? Must be that bag your good-for-nothin' brother is carryin'. That an' the expectant look on his face. Looks like he's hopin' to stay.'

'Won't be no trouble, I promise,' Drew said.

'Trouble follows you around like the stink on a skunk, Drew,' his aunt said. 'Even your mother admitted that before she died.'

Drew's face coloured with anger, but

he managed to control himself. 'You won't know I'm here.'

'I-I'll make sure he behaves, Aunt Bella,' Kate said.

'What was wrong with the hotel?' Aunt Bella asked. 'They throw you out for not payin' your bill?'

'N-o-o,' Drew answered carefully. 'I just thought it'd be nice to be with *family* for a while.'

Aunt Bella sniffed but said nothing for several moments. At last she turned to Kate. 'Think I'll go on up to bed, Kate. Maybe then he'll tell you the real reason he's come. Then again, maybe he won't.'

They waited until she had left the room, then Kate turned on her brother. 'Right, let's have it. And don't try fobbing me off with some lie, I want the truth.'

Drew dropped his bag on the floor and slumped into the seat his aunt had vacated.

'Seems another of the Cotton gang survived besides me,' he said. 'An' he's the nastiest of the bunch with a quick temper.'

Kate stared at him. 'You told me they'd all been killed.'

'Seems I was wrong. Curtis Jordan escaped, an' he's come lookin' for me. Wants his share of the money.'

'So give it to him. In fact, give him *all* the money. It's poison, Drew, and we don't need it.'

'*I* need it. 'Sides,' he said, sheepishly, 'there ain't much more'n half of it left.'

'Then give him that.'

'Ain't that simple, Sis. He won't be too pleased I high-tailed it after the robbery. He's gonna kill me, Kate. That's why I'm here. I need somewhere to hole up for a few days.'

'You aren't thinking straight,' she said. 'As soon as he finds out you've got a sister and that I'm living here, it will be the first place he'll come looking. You can't stay.'

'OK, then I'll move on tomorrow!' he snapped.

'At first light,' Kate told him. 'But

where will you go?'

'Anywhere, just so long as it's a long way from here. When I've settled someplace, I'll wire you.'

'Maybe you should go to the sheriff,' she said. 'Give yourself up and hand over what's left of the money; and tell him about this Curtis Jordan so that the law can take care of him.'

'Now it's you who ain't thinkin' straight. You want to see me go to prison for the rest of my life? Maybe hang? Why — ' He stopped, suddenly realizing he'd said too much.

Kate was white-faced. '*Hang*? Drew, you told me nobody was hurt, only the gang members.'

He stayed silent, not meeting her eyes. She reached out and grabbed his arm. '*Tell me!*'

'I killed a man,' he said after a moment. 'I had to, Kate, he was going for a gun! Likely he would've killed me!' It was stretching the truth, but he didn't care. 'Would you rather I was dead?'

'No, of course not, but — '

'Then quit lookin' at me like that,' he snapped.

'So what are you going to do?'

'I don't know, but I'll think of somethin'. Go to bed. I'll be gone afore you're up.'

Kate stared at him for some moments. He was her younger brother, but suddenly she realized that she didn't know him any more. She had promised her dying mother that she would look after him, try and keep him on the straight and narrow, but he'd gone too far this time, killing a man.

'Go to bed, Sis,' he told her again.

She nodded. 'Guess I will.' She put out a hand and touched his cheek. 'Oh, *Drew*.'

Drew listened to her mounting the stairs to her bedroom. Already a plan was forming in his mind. He had no intention of giving away one cent of the money, or of leaving Latimer.

At least, not until he'd put a bullet in Curtis Jordan.

18

Curtis got himself a room at the Bib 'n Tucker bar. It wasn't much bigger than a livery stall, and contained only a cot and a blanket, but after two days of hard riding, he would have bedded down on a dirt floor if needs be.

He woke late. There was a washroom at the end of the passage, where he splashed water over his hands and face, then he went out into the street to find someplace to get breakfast.

He came across the Eating House some minutes later. The smell of frying bacon attacked his nostrils as he pushed open the door.

The place was half-full, and Curtis found himself a table in a corner, back to the wall, facing the door. A pretty young waitress came across.

'Ham'n eggs, wheat toast an' coffee,' he told her.

'Yes, sir,' she said.

Was he imagining it, or was she looking at him more warily than a stranger's presence warranted?

'Somethin' botherin' you?' he asked.

'No, sir,' she said quickly, and scuttled off.

A few minutes later, she returned with his breakfast. She placed the plate and mug in front of him and turned to leave. He put a hand on her wrist, gripping it firmly.

'I'm lookin' for someone,' he said. 'Name of Drew Hudson. You know him?'

She shook her head, her eyes wide with fright.

'Reckon you do,' he said.

'No!' She turned her head, looking for help.

Curtis stared at her for a moment, then released her wrist. 'OK,' he said slowly.

He watched her hurry away towards the kitchen, then attacked his food.

'Reckon she was lyin',' he muttered to himself, 'but she'll keep.'

In the kitchen, Bella had been watching through the serving hatch.

'That him?' she asked Kate when the girl returned.

Kate nodded. 'It must be.'

'What'd you tell him?'

'Nothing,' Kate said. 'He asked me if I knew Drew, I said no.'

'Likely he didn't believe you, seein' as you look like a scared rabbit. Probably didn't want to make a scene in here, though.'

Bella had coaxed the truth out of her niece that morning, after discovering that Drew had flown the coop. She had been shocked to hear that the young fool had been involved in a bank robbery and had killed a man, yet when she thought about it, it wasn't too surprising, the way the young hellion had been going these past few months.

'Once he starts askin' around, he's gonna find out sooner or later that you're Drew's sister,' she said. 'Maybe it's best to come clean about who you are, but tell him that you ain't got any idea where your brother's gone. Distance yourself from the little tearaway. It's somethin' you should have done a long time ago, Kate.'

'Ma asked me — '

'Yeah, I know what she asked you,' Bella cut in. 'But she didn't know what sort of a burden she was layin' on you. He's goin' to come to a bad end, that brother of yours. I just don't want you to be goin' down with him.' She wiped her hands on her apron. 'Leave it to me. You stay in here. I'm gonna go have a word with Mister Curtis Jordan.'

★　★　★

Curtis was finishing the last of his coffee when the large woman he'd seen emerge from the kitchen with a steaming jug, poured him a second mug.

'Bella Gower,' she announced. 'I own this place.'

'Yeah?' Curtis said.

'Seems my niece — that's the young lady who served you — might've misled you.'

Curtis smiled crookedly. 'Figured as much.'

'You made her nervous.'

'Yeah? But I don't scare you.'

Bella shook her head. 'Not much does nowadays. Anyway, the man you're lookin' for is her brother.'

'Drew Hudson,' Curtis said.

'Right. Well, he's gone. Left town early this mornin'. Guess he knew you'd come lookin' for him.'

'You know *why* I'm lookin' for him?'

'He owes you some money.'

'A whole heap of money,' Curtis agreed.

'Suppose he gave it to you. Would you leave him alone then?'

He stared at her, picking a sliver of ham from between his teeth with his thumbnail, then shook his head slowly. 'Nobody double-crosses me an' gets away with it, Bella.'

'That's what I thought,' Bella said.

'Anyways, just so you understand. Me an' Kate have got no idea where Drew's gone. That clear?'

Curtis sipped his coffee. 'Sure,' he said. He delved into his pocket for some money.

'On the house,' Bella said.

He smiled his crooked smile. 'Well, that's right neighbourly of you, Bella.'

'Be glad if you ate someplace else if you plan stayin' in town,' she said. 'Not that there's much point in you stayin'. Drew'll be miles from here by now.'

'You know what?' he said. 'I ain't so sure about that. Wouldn't surprise me if'n he's holed up somewhere, waitin' for a chance to back-shoot me. That way he'd keep the money for himself.'

Bella Gower didn't reply, but he could see he'd sown the seed of doubt in her mind.

'We've got a diligent sheriff in Latimer,' she told him. 'Reckon he'd be interested to hear there was a member of the Cotton gang in town. The gang who raided the bank in Suta Springs.'

Curtis grinned. 'You can't prove any of that, Bella. Me, a member of the Cotton gang? Why, that's only rumours. My face ain't on no law dodger. As for a bank raid in Suta Springs, you got proof I was involved, other than what that lyin' nephew of yours told you? I reckon not. 'Sides, even if you could prove I took part in the raid, you think I wouldn't put the sheriff on to Drew? 'Course I would, an' when they caught him, he'd hang! Nope, you ain't goin' to no sheriff, Bella Gower.'

He pushed his chair back and rose from the table.

He winked at her. 'I'll be seein' you.'

★   ★   ★

'Do you think he's right?' Kate asked her aunt a few minutes later. 'Do you think Drew is still in town, waiting to — to do what that man said?'

'Don't know what to think,' Bella said. 'Maybe Drew's fool enough, but I hope to God he ain't.'

She began crashing around with pots and pans. Kate watched her, knowing that the other woman was trying to put the business of Drew and his problems out of her mind.

'I'm sorry I brought this on you, Aunt Bella,' she said.

Bella stopped what she was doing and put an arm round her niece. 'Ain't your fault, honey. Don't worry, we'll get through this fine.' But there was little conviction in her voice.

Kate tried to smile. 'Sure,' she said. 'Sure we will.'

19

'You can't stay cooped up here for ever,' Lottie said. 'Opal'll get suspicious.'

She was sitting cross-legged on the bed in her underwear, watching Drew. He was standing to one side of the window of her room, looking out into the street, a worried expression on his face.

'Opal didn't see me come up here.'

'Don't matter whether she did or not. She'll know I'm occupied with somebody, an' she'll get to wonderin' what's happenin' after an hour or so. Prob'ly come up an' see who's here.'

'So I'll tell her I've paid for the mornin', aft'noon an' evenin'. Quit worryin', Lottie.'

'Seems to me it's you who's worried. That fella still lookin' for you?'

He didn't answer.

'What's he gonna do if'n he sees you?'

'Nothin', if I see him first.'

'Why, what you gonna do to him?'

Again, he didn't answer, and Lottie drew her own conclusions.

'You're gonna kill him, ain't you?'

'Lottie, quit talkin', will you?' Drew moved away from the window and joined her on the bed. He sat glowering and chewing his fingernail.

Lottie grinned and started to unbutton his shirt. 'You ready, lover-boy?'

After a moment, Drew grinned back. 'Guess I might as well pass the time pleasurably.'

Ten minutes later they were writhing naked on the bed when the door burst open and Opal Harris's fat form waddled in.

'Oh, so it is you, is it?' she said, addressing Drew's naked buttocks.

'*Judas*, Opal!' Drew yelled. 'Ain't you ever heard of knockin'?'

'Not when it's my house, I ain't,' she told him. 'Anyways, I gotta message for you.'

Drew rolled off Lottie, covering

himself as best he could with his hands. 'Message?'

'Seems there's some fella lookin' for you.' She followed this with an all-too-accurate description of Curtis Jordan.

'You didn't tell him I was here, did you?' The panic in Drew's voice was palpable.

'Nope,' Opal said. 'Discretion bein' my middle name. Anyways, I wasn't sure it was you with Lottie, not until I'd checked.' She smiled a crooked smile. 'Reckon you owe me, Drew Hudson.'

'Yeah, OK,' he said. 'Now d'you mind clearin' out so's a fella can get dressed?'

'Sure,' Opal said, grinning. 'Course, if you want to stay for the rest of the night, that's OK by me, as long as you pay your way.'

'What d'you mean?' he said.

'Let's call it five hundred dollars, shall we?' Opal said. 'It's a nice round figure.'

'*Five hundred?*' Drew's face darkened with anger. 'That's blackmail!'

The grin vanished from Opal's face.

'Take it or leave it. Remember, you're buyin' my silence, Lottie's too. Could be we're lettin' ourselves in for a whole heap of trouble hidin' you here. That gunslinger looked a nasty piece of work.'

Drew fumed but gave in. 'OK,' he said. 'Send up some food and a bottle of whiskey — no charge!'

Opal nodded. 'Sure thing.' She looked at Lottie and grinned. 'Guess you can put your clothes on, Lottie. You're client's ardour seems to have shrunk a little!' And she left the room laughing.

20

It was late evening when Clayton rode into Latimer, saddle-sore and hungry. Had Curtis put up at the hotel? Probably not. Clayton reckoned the gunslinger was more likely to find a saloon where he could enjoy the company of a soiled dove or two and a supply of whiskey on tap. Speaking of which, Clayton's mouth was drier than a desert rock.

Chances were, Curtis had found himself a place in the town's red-light district, so Clayton headed for that area after checking his horse in at a livery and taking a room at the Prime Hotel.

He stopped at the first saloon he came across, anxious to slake his thirst. The place had the sign Opal's House on its fascia board. He pushed his way through the batwings and crossed to the bar.

'Beer and a red-eye chaser,' he told the

barkeep. 'An' make me a beef sandwich.'

Several drinks later, he began making enquiries.

'You know an *hombre* with the name Drew Hudson?' he asked the barkeep.

'Hudson? Nope,' the barkeep said. But he was avoiding Clayton's eye.

Clayton removed a gold eagle from his waistcoat pocket and began to flip it with his thumb and finger. 'You sure about that?'

The barkeep — a short, stubby man with a walrus moustache and a horse-shoe of hair round his otherwise bald head — glanced across the room at the vast figure of a woman whose breasts were in danger of exploding out of the top of her silk dress. Clayton guessed it was the owner of the establishment. Having established that he was not being watched or overheard, the barkeep leaned towards Clayton and lowered his voice.

'Top of the stairs, second door on the right,' he said.

With that, he moved away and began polishing a glass.

Unable to believe his luck at finding Hudson so quickly, Clayton moved casually towards the staircase. Like the barkeep, he checked that the fat lady's attention was occupied elsewhere. Seeing that it was, he sprinted up the stairs two at a time.

He hesitated outside the appropriate door, debating whether or not to knock; decided surprise might be the best tactic, and strode in.

Drew Hudson was slumped on a sofa by the window, sound asleep. A girl was sitting partially clothed on the bed, reading a penny dreadful novel. Her mouth dropped open when she saw Clayton.

'What . . . ?' she began.

He put a finger to his lips. 'Shhh,' he told her. 'What's your name?'

The girl continued to stare at him, fear in her eyes.

'Lottie,' she whispered.

Clayton nodded and smiled reassuringly. Then he walked across and gently shook the sleeping man's shoulder. Drew stirred and opened his eyes. He stared at Clayton as if he'd seen a ghost.

'Evenin', Drew,' Clayton said.

'Chandler!' Drew leapt to his feet. 'How the hell . . . ?'

'Long story,' Clayton said. 'Want to hear it?'

Drew's face paled. 'If it's the money you're after, there ain't that much left. Anyways, Wolf's dead, so your bettin' marker's history, Clayton. An' you don't owe me anythin'.'

'I know that,' Clayton said.

'So why've you come after me?'

'The bank manager you shot an' killed was my pa's best friend,' Clayton said. 'An' the woman Curtis ran down an' killed was my sister-in-law. So my pa wants you an' Curtis dead, an' he sent me after you. Of course, he don't know about my part in the bank raid, an' that's the way I want it to stay.'

'Sure, sure,' Drew said. 'Ain't no need to kill me. I can keep my mouth shut.'

Clayton put a hand on the kid's

shoulder. 'Fact is, Drew, you ruined everythin' when you got trigger-happy.'

'Jeeze, Clayton, I'm sorry. I just got scared.' Drew put his head in his hands. 'I should never have got mixed up with Wolf Cotton. I ain't no gunslinger. Ain't no bank robber either. An' now Curtis is after me. He's in town, did you know that? If'n he finds me, I'm dead meat, that's for sure.'

'So we need to find him first,' Clayton said, an idea forming in his head. 'Listen, Drew, I'm on your side. We can work together. And with Curtis dead, there's no chance of my pa finding out about my part in the robbery.'

'He wouldn't come after me?'

'I'd tell him Curtis killed you first.'

A gleam of hope appeared in Drew's eyes. 'It might work,' he allowed. 'Yeah, it might.'

' 'Course, I'd want a share of what's left of the money,' Clayton said.

'Sure, Clayton,' Drew said, eagerly. ' 'Course, it ain't here. I got it hidden someplace. But we'll split it down the middle. Fifty-fifty.'

Clayton smiled to himself.

Fifty-fifty? No, kid. I'm taking all of it.

Killing Curtis would be easier with Drew as bait to catch the gunslinger off guard, Clayton thought. Then, with Curtis out of the way, finishing off Drew Hudson would be child's play. As the kid had just admitted, he was no gunman.

But there was the little matter of the bank money. Clayton didn't believe that it was almost all gone. And OK, so his slate with Wolf Cotton had been wiped clean now the gang leader was dead, but it would be good to come out of this mess with *something*. Nine or ten thousand dollars would buy him some independence from his father. Give him an opportunity to get away from the Double C, strike out on his own someplace else. He'd always hated ranching. Maybe he could become a professional gambler, plying his trade on the riverboats that steamed up and down the

Mississippi. It was a lifestyle that appealed to him.

But for the moment he would have to play Drew along. Feign a friendship until he could find out where the money was stashed.

'First we have to find him,' Clayton said.

'That's easy,' Drew said. 'He's stayin' across the street in the Bib'n Tucker.'

Clayton looked at him quickly. 'He is? How d'you know?'

'I seen him goin' in an' out. That's why I'm stayin' here with Lottie. It's a good vantage point.'

Clayton glanced back at the girl on the bed. She had been giving the appearance of ignoring the two of them but Clayton knew she had been listening to every word.

'How long were you plannin' to stay here?' he asked Drew.

'Until Curtis got tired of lookin' for me, or decided I'd moved on, an' he left,' Drew replied.

Clayton thought for a moment, then

said, 'He's got to find you before that. You've got to let him see you. Get him to chase you into a blind alley, where I'll be hidden. Then I'll kill him.'

Drew looked alarmed. He didn't like the idea of being bait. 'What if'n he kills me straight out, without botherin' to chase me?'

'He won't,' Clayton said. 'He'll want to get his hands on the bank money first. He doesn't know where you've hidden it.'

And neither do I.

Drew chewed it over in his mind for some minutes. At last he said, 'OK, when do we do it?'

'Tonight,' Clayton told him. 'Now, I need to know exactly where you're gonna lead him so that I can get there ahead of time an' find a place to hide.'

Drew nodded. 'I know just the place.'

21

Curtis Jordan was in a foul temper. All day he'd paced the streets of Latimer hoping for a sight Drew Hudson, but without success. Nobody he'd spoken to seemed to have any idea where the kid might be holed up, or if they had, they'd been unwilling to tell him.

He sat at a table in the corner of the Bib'n Tucker bar nursing a bottle of red-eye and flipping cards in a half-hearted attempt at solitaire. His room upstairs was less than welcoming, but he decided to finish the bottle and head for his bed.

It was at that moment his luck appeared to change. For who should be peering over the top of the batwings but the very young man he'd been hunting all day!

Drew Hudson seemed cautious as he surveyed the scene. When his eyes lit on

Curtis, they widened with fright and he turned and ran.

Curtis was out of his chair with such speed that he sent the cards flying and the bottle spinning to the stone floor, where it smashed.

Gasper Row was Latimer's red-light district's main thoroughfare. Light spilled from the doorways of bars and cathouses; honky-tonk music came from the saloons. By the time Curtis got out into the thick of it, he was just in time to see Drew disappearing into a sidestreet fifty yeards away on the opposite side of the Row. Curtis bounded after him, brushing aside anyone who blocked his way.

The sidestreet led into a maze of alleyways and passages, all of them poorly lit or pitch black. For the most part Curtis had to rely on moonlight to see where he was going. However, his eyes soon became accustomed to the semi-darkness and he managed to keep the shadowy form of his prey in view.

At last, his quarry turned into a